Percy Bysshe Shelley, Albert S. Cook

A Defense of Poetry

Percy Bysshe Shelley, Albert S. Cook

A Defense of Poetry

ISBN/EAN: 9783337777586

Printed in Europe, USA, Canada, Australia, Japan

Cover: Foto ©Andreas Hilbeck / pixelio.de

More available books at **www.hansebooks.com**

A Defense of Poetry is the only entirely finished prose work Shelley left. In this we find the reverence with which he regarded his art. We discern his power of close reasoning, and the unity of his views of human nature. The language is imaginative, but not flowery; the periods have an intonation full of majesty and grace; and the harmony of the style being united to melodious thought, a music results, that swells upon the ear, and fills the mind with delight.

MRS. SHELLEY, Preface to *Essays, etc., by Percy Bysshe Shelley.*

To prefer or to equal Shelley's prose to his poetry is a merely uncritical freak of judgment. His prose is, however, of excellent quality, both in his letters, which are among the most charming of their kind, and in his too few essays and miscellaneous writings.

SAINTSBURY, *Specimens of English Prose Style*, p. 342.

The mere whim, the bare idea, that poetry is a deep thing, a teaching thing, the most surely and wisely elevating of human things, is even now to the coarse public mind nearly unknown. . . . All about and around us a faith in poetry struggles to be extricated, but it is not extricated. Some day, at the touch of the true word, the whole confusion will by magic cease; the broken and shapeless notions will cohere and crystallize into a bright and true theory.

BAGEHOT, *Literary Studies*, 2. 339–341.

Shelley

A DEFENSE OF POETRY

EDITED

WITH INTRODUCTION AND NOTES

BY

ALBERT S. COOK

PROFESSOR OF THE ENGLISH LANGUAGE AND LITERATURE
IN YALE UNIVERSITY

BOSTON, U.S.A.

PUBLISHED BY GINN & COMPANY

1891

TYPOGRAPHY BY J. S. CUSHING & CO., BOSTON, U.S.A.

PRESSWORK BY GINN & CO., BOSTON, U.S.A.

CONTENTS.

v

INTRODUCTION.

1. STYLE.

SHELLEY'S prose, though by no means excessively cadenced or adorned, has yet some of the marks and qualities of poetry. It can scarcely be called poetic prose, as much of Ruskin's might not unfairly be styled ; nor does it answer in all respects to the accepted notions of a poet's prose. Perhaps its characteristic has been sufficiently defined by himself in his own discussion of the 'vulgar error' that prose can never be the vehicle of an essentially poetic conception. In this discussion he does not shrink from definite statements and concrete examples (9 8-31) : " Plato was essentially a poet—the truth and splendor of his imagery, and the melody of his language, are the most intense that it is possible to conceive. . . . He forbore to invent any regular plan of rhythm which would include, under determinate forms, the varied pauses of his style. Cicero sought to imitate the cadence of his periods, but with little success. Lord Bacon was a poet. His language has a sweet and majestic rhythm which satisfies the sense. . . . All the authors of revolution in opinion are not only necessarily poets as they are inventors, . . . but as their periods are harmonious and rhythmical."

The author himself has thus enunciated two criteria which may be applied to the prose written by a poet or in a poetic mood :

1. Truth and splendor of imagery.

2. Melody or rhythm, varied, — indeterminate, and inimitable.

That Shelley's prose imagery possesses both truth and splendor there can be no question. Mrs. Shelley, surely not an incompetent critic, distinctly attributes to his language both the qualities just mentioned, and it needs no exhaustive scrutiny to determine that for these qualities his language is chiefly indebted to its figurative expressions. In the preface to her edition of his essays, she says : "Shelley commands language splendid and melodious as Plato."

The imagery of this essay always completes, if it does not effect, the revelation of its author's thought. A mind of more prosaic temper might attain equal clearness without the employment of metaphorical language, but clearness may in such cases be gained at the expense of suggestiveness. There is a creeping clearness, as there is a volant amplitude of vision, no less certain than that of the eagle when he swoops magnificently down upon his prey from the central deeps of air. It is the latter that Shelley possesses, and herein he reminds us of Shakespeare when the great dramatist is most felicitous in wedding virile thought to the clinging beauty of tropical language. In Agamemnon's speech to his auxiliar kings, Shakespeare makes him thus eloquently illustrate a commonplace heroic : —

> Why then, you princes,
> Do you with cheeks abashed behold our works,
> And think them shames, which are indeed nought else
> But the protractive trials of great Jove,
> To find persistive constancy in men?
> The fineness of which metal is not found
> In fortune's love; for then the bold and coward,
> The wise and fool, the artist and unread,
> The hard and soft, seem all affined and kin;
> But, in the wind and tempest of her frown,
> Distinction, with a broad and powerful fan,
> Puffing at all, winnows the light away;
> And what hath mass or matter by itself
> Lies rich in virtue and unmingled.

Now it is no sufficient objection to the dramatist's use of figurative language to say that all this expenditure of words is but the amplification of a single short sentence, " Adversity distinguishes the hero from the poltroon." Nor is it an answer to say that such introduction of metaphor is suitable to poetry, but not to prose, else what censure must be pronounced on such an evident metaphor as this, " Whose fan is in his hand, and he will thoroughly purge his floor, and gather his wheat into the garner ; but he will burn up the chaff with unquenchable fire ? " We praise the aptness, as well as the beauty, of Jeremy Taylor's famous simile : " For so have I seen a lark rising from his bed of grass, soaring upwards and singing as he rises and hopes to get to heaven and climb above the clouds ; but the poor bird was beaten back with the loud sighings of an eastern wind and his motion made irregular and inconstant, descending more at every breath of the tempest than it could recover by the vibration and frequent weighing of his wings, till the little creature was forced to sit down and pant and stay till the storm was over ; and then it made a prosperous flight and did rise and sing as if it had learned music and motion from an angel as he passed sometimes through the air about his ministries here below. So is the prayer of a good man," etc. But if we admire the fitness of this image, there is no room left for us to condemn the not dissimilar expressions of Shelley : " The world, as from a resurrection, balancing itself on the golden wings of knowledge and of hope, has reassumed its yet unwearied flight into the heaven of time. Listen to the music, unheard by outward ears, which is as a ceaseless and invisible wind, nourishing its everlasting course with strength and swiftness."

But, indeed, there is no necessity of defending figurative language on the score of its services to truth, so long as we can appeal to the example of England's most philosophical politician. Burke, in his *Letter to a Noble Lord*, does not shrink from the employment of a trope hardly less elaborate than those that have just been cited, and no one has yet been bold enough to censure him for temerity, or to insinuate that he could more exactly have conveyed his thought by eschewing the ornaments of verse. Rising to the demands of the occasion, Burke says : " But as to our country and our race, as long as the well-compacted structure of our church and state, the sanctuary, the holy of holies of that ancient law, defended by reverence, defended by power, a fortress at once and a temple, shall stand inviolate on the brow of the British Sion — as long as the British monarchy, not more limited than fenced by the orders of the state, shall, like the proud Keep of Windsor, rising in the majesty of proportion, and girt with the double belt of its kindred and coeval towers, as long as this awful structure shall over-see and guard the subjected land — so long the mounds and dykes of the low, fat Bedford level will have nothing to fear from all the pickaxes of all the levelers of France."

Is Shelley's imagery splendid? If not splendid, it is at least generally beautiful, and bears an obvious resemblance to that of his poetry. Many of his illustrations are drawn from light, fire, the wind, music, birds, and flowers. It would be an agreeable and instructive task to make a collection of his metaphorical phrases, to trace his indebtedness to the Bible and other classics, and to spell out the character of his genius in the light of his similes, but we cannot afford our-selves the indulgence in this place.

We pass now to the second head, that of melody or rhythm. The inference from his words is that the rhythm of a poet's prose is inimitable, *because* varied and indeterminate. Varied and indeterminate it may be, but no less unmistakable. The melody of Shelley's language, if not " the most intense that it is possible to conceive," is sufficiently intense to differen-tiate it from ordinary, plodding, work-a-day prose, and to seem, as indeed it is, " an echo of the eternal music." This melody is heard at its best in sentences like the following : —

" The Past, like an inspired rhapsodist, fills the theatre of everlasting generations with their harmony."

" Its secret alchemy turns to potable gold the poisonous waters which flow from death through life." (Perhaps suggested by such Shakespearean lines as *M.N.D.* 3. 2. 391 : " Turns into yellow gold his salt green streams "; *Sonn.* 33. 3 : " Gilding pale streams with heavenly alchemy"; *K. John* 3. 1. 77, etc.).

Still more striking than these are the two sentences cited on p. 1.

It will be observed that sentences of this order have a sustained flight, like that of the bird of paradise, which is fabled never to touch the earth, or rather, if we may adapt Jeremy Taylor's simile, already quoted, like the impulsive soaring of the lark, which ever and anon returns to the meadow whence it sprang, and does not at once shake itself free of its lowly surroundings, but which exults in its spacious liberty when the earth has fairly been left behind, and with glad pulsations lifts itself higher and higher into the immeasurable profound of air. Sentences like those quoted above, when examined with reference to their pauses, are seen to have no natural cæsura near the end. They spring through a short clause, or a succession of them, to a coign of vantage, and thence set out on an aërial journey which halts not till it ends. No antithesis marks their close, no qualifying clause slipped in almost at the last moment, no suspension which throws the verb, with an abrupt break, to the very end, no explicative remark intended merely to confirm or extend that which precedes, no correlative added for the sake of more perfect balance. Examples of such broken endings might readily be adduced, and I select from Ruskin's *Sesame and Lilies* an instance to illustrate each of the foregoing heads : —

"Strong always to sanctify, even when they cannot save."

"A broken metaphor, one might think, careless and un-scholarly."

"And sown in us daily, and by us, as instantly as may be, choked."   .

"Only so far as may enable her to sympathize in her husband's pleasures, and in those of his best friends."

"We gloat over the pathos of the police court, and gather the night-dew of the grave."

It is impossible to lay down any rule for the construction of prose rhythms. If such a rule could be deduced, the rhythm would no longer be varied and indeterminate. Still an examination of the final sentences of Shelley's paragraphs is instructive with reference to the means by which the continuous harmony is so long maintained. When the final clause exceeds the ordinary length and is interrupted by no appreciable cæsura, it will frequently be found that it contains a succession of two or more prepositional phrases, more rarely that the place of the first prepositional phrase is occupied by a noun, the subject or object of a verb, with or without one or more attributive adjectives, or that the second prepositional phrase is adverbial in its function. Nor is it alone in the *final* sentences of Shelley's paragraphs that such constructions appear to be typical. Other instances are : —

"Become as generals to the bewildered armies of their thoughts."

"And gathers a sort of reduplication from the community."

"It must be impanelled by Time from the selectest of the wise of many generations."

"The receptacle of a thousand unapprehended combinations of thought."

"To have abdicated this throne of their widest dominion."

"Out of a chaos of inharmonious barbarisms."

But the moment a serious attempt is made to establish the universality of such a supposed rule, that moment disappointment is likely to overtake the observer, and to nip in the bud any future endeavors to determine even the most elementary laws of verbal harmony in prose. Yet, confined within proper limits, such endeavors need not be unprofitable ; they should be judged in the light of the inquiries, extending over centuries, and still continued, into the rhythms of Lysias and Demosthenes, and it should not be hastily concluded that what is advantageous in Greek becomes a vanity and a delusion in English.

Shelley's attachment to a few favorite images leads him, as has been already intimated, into repetition. As the most intricate musical compositions are built up out of the few notes of the scale, so poets, even when writing prose, appear to have a few simple elements to which they frequently return, and to vary and modulate upon a few primary chords. Among Shelley's key-words are ' harmony,' ' harmonious,' ' rhythm,' ' order or rhythm,' ' rhythm and order.' Akin to this practice, but yet different from it, is that of repeating certain syllables or sounds, simply because the echo of them still lingers in the ear. Whether Shelley's use of the figure of polysyndeton, especially in the case of ' and,' is to be referred to this cause, may be allowed to remain an open question. But other instances are less doubtful, and can only be regarded as blemishes, since they transgress a higher euphonic law. Such are : —

" *Film* of *famil*iarity (42 16).

" *Affect*ed a moral aim, and the *effect* of their poetry " (15 2).

" An equal *sens*ibility to the influ*ence* of the *sens*es " (21 30).

" As its *forms* survived in the unre*form*ed worship of modern Europe " (32 18).

But especially the multiplication of words ending in the

sound of -*sion*, preceded by a vowel, such as the following : —

" The incorpora*tion* of the Celtic *nations* with the exhausted popula*tion* " (27 26).

" He omits the observa*tion* of cond*itions* still more important, and more is lost than gained by the substit*ution* of
the rigidly-defined and ever-repeated idealisms of a distorted
superst*ition* for the loving impersona*tions* of the truth of
human *passion*" (17 25–30) ; cf. Sidney, *Defense* 53 31, note.

Another form of repetition is that of identical words, such
as 'alleged' (31 4, 7), 'practice' (17 3, 4).   Not to be confounded with these are such as *selectest*: *selectest* (23 28),
and *partial*: *partially* (24 1, 2), which illustrate a rhetorical
device.

Alliteration in prose is due to the same retention and unconscious reverberation of a sound, this time fragmentary
and initial, a single phonetic element instead of a group of
such.   Shelley does not escape this fault, or rather he in-
dulges a common and pardonable propensity beyond the
limits which are imposed by the severe taste of certain
critics.   " The mask and the mantle " (30 5) would almost
pass unnoticed, and " the fragrance of all the flowers of the
field " (21 20) can be readily condoned.   But the following
will not so easily escape remark : —

" It overcomes and *s*ickens the *s*pirit with ex*c*ess of *s*weet-
ness " (21 17).

" A *m*onologue, where all the attention may be directed
to some great *m*aster of ideal *m*imicry.   The *m*odern practice," etc. (17 1).

" The *j*ury which sits in *j*udgment upon a *p*oet must be
com*p*osed of his *p*eers ; it must be im*p*anelled by Time. . . .
A poet is a nightingale, who *s*its in darkness and *s*ings to
cheer its own *s*olitude with *s*weet *s*ounds ; his auditors are
as *m*en entranced by the *m*elody of an unseen *m*usician, who
feel that they are *m*oved," etc. (11 27–12 2).   Perhaps the

misquotation in 35 27-8 owes its form to the instinct for alliteration, and ' feasting ' becomes ' mirth,' because ' mourning ' had preceded.

One feature of a poetical style Shelley avoids, the introduction of compound words, such as Sidney loved and abounded in (cf. Sidney, *Defense* 55 25, note, and the Introduction, pp. xxiv–xxv). A half-dozen practically exhaust the list : ' all-penetrating ' (46 22), ' ever-changing ' (2 6), ' ever-repeated ' (17 28), ' low-thoughted ' (45 31), ' many-sided ' (19 6), and ' owl-eyed ' (39 4). Of these, ' low-thoughted ' is a quotation, and ' owl-winged ' is the only other that has a decidedly poetic air.

Before leaving the subject of Shelley's style, a single defect and a compensating merit must be noticed. The defect is that the poet as prosaist is sometimes ungrammatical. The congruence of a verb with its subject, for example, is not always observed. Examples are : —

" As the temporary dress . . . , which *cover* without concealing," etc. (12 29).

" With which the author, in common with his auditors, *are* infected " (19 22).

" The chosen delicacy of expressions . . . *are* as a mist," etc. (24 5).

" His apotheosis of Beatrice, and the gradations . . . *is* the most glorious imagination of modern poetry " (29 3-8).

" After one person and one age *has* exhausted all its divine effluence which *their* peculiar relations enable *them* to share," etc. (33 10-12).

" The accumulation of the materials of external life *exceed*," etc. (38 11).

The verbal noun uniformly takes an object : " The establishing a relation," etc. (17 23 ; cf. 17 24, 34 12-15).

A peculiar confusion is illustrated by the following : " *Each* division in the art *was* made perfect . . . , and was disciplined into a beautiful proportion and unity *one towards the other* " (16 17-20).

The connective *as* here does duty in a construction to which it is not perfectly adapted : " Never was blind strength and stubborn form *so* disciplined . . . , or that will *less* repugnant, . . . *as* during the century," etc. (15 17-21).

In the following the second member of the compound sentence is left without a verb : " Tragedy becomes a cold imitation . . . ; and often the very form misunderstood, or a weak attempt to teach certain doctrines," etc. (19 14 ff.). ' Form ' and ' attempt ' simulate noun-subjects, but the close of the sentence leaves them suspended, as it were, in midair.

These offences, it will be said, are venial, and so indeed they are in relation to the splendid qualities by which they are offset, but the reference to them may perhaps serve as an excuse for occasional lapses in our elder writers, as where Sidney says (*Defense* 47 28) : " Our tragedies and comedies not without cause cried out against," etc., in which the finite verb is lacking.

The counterbalancing, and more than counterbalancing, merit, is the apothegmatic character of many of Shelley's statements. Perhaps no English essay so flowing and easy in its style, and so brief in its compass, ever contained an equally large number of pregnant sayings, so excellently true and so adequately expressed. Two, at least, have become proverbial : " Poetry is the record of the best and happiest moments of the happiest and best minds." " The rich have become richer, and the poor poorer." But there is a large number scarcely less deserving of popular currency. A few of these may be instanced : —

" A poem is the very image of life expressed in its eternal truth."

" It is not what the erotic poets have, but what they have not, in which their imperfection consists."

" A man, to be greatly good, must imagine intensely and comprehensively."

" Man, having enslaved the elements, remains himself a slave."

" For the end of social corruption is to destroy all sensibility to pleasure ; and therefore it is corruption."

"Tragedy delights by affording a shadow of that pleasure which exists in pain."

" All high poetry is infinite ; it is as the first acorn, which contains all oaks potentially."

But to continue to quote would be to repeat the Essay in the Introduction.

2. SHELLEY'S VIEWS IN COMPARISON WITH SIDNEY'S.

In essentials Shelley and Sidney agree. Both being poets, and acquainted with the same early literatures and authorities, it might be expected that their views would not be widely divergent. Among the opinions which they hold in common, only the principal need be mentioned.

According to both, then, poetry is the first of didactic agencies, in time as well as in order of importance, and, to descend to particulars, outranks both history and philosophy, each of which, in its infancy, embodies something of its great predecessor. It is true that the philosophy which Sidney has in mind is ethics, while Shelley is thinking rather of political science, but this difference is merely indicative of the period ; that which was academic and general in the sixteenth century had become democratic and specifically sociological by the beginning of the nineteenth. Again, while they pronounce poetry to be the first of didactic agencies, neither writer will allow that the poetry which studiously and incessantly reminds us of its moral aim has a right to a place among the highest.

They agree that there is something prophetic about poetry ; the poet has the " vision and the faculty divine." Accordingly there is much poetry in the Bible. Moreover, the insight of the true seer cannot be acquired through scholastic discipline ; there is a sense in which the poet must be born to his lofty mission.

It is not necessary that poetry take the form of verse, although, since harmony is the soul of poetry, numbers constitute the usual and fitting body to this soul. Plato is instanced by both as a prose-poet, or, if the phrase be preferred, as a prosaist whose substance is poetical.

Again, poetic art improves upon nature ; the world of the poet is a fairer one than was ever seen by mortal eye, and hence his imagined world may well become the foundation of the actual one, — the type which men seek to realize. Not only is such endeavor at realization possible, but, as an historical fact, men have taken the figments of the poets for models, Homer being an instance in point. The truth revealed by poetry is infinitely attractive, but can only be seen by ordinary men in the creations of the bard ; the latter are therefore true in the deepest sense, and fictitious only in the superficial one. Finally, the test of poetry is its delightfulness in combination with its didactic efficacy and elevation ; let it fail of either, and it must at once be consigned to a lower rank as poetry, or be denied that name altogether ; —

> Omne tulit punctum qui miscuit utile dulci
> Lectorem delectando pariterque monendo.

Notwithstanding a concurrence of view extending to so many particulars, it must not be inferred that Shelley's essay is a mere reproduction of Sidney's. Even in poetic endowment they were unlike, and no less in education and temperament. Sidney was trained in a severer school than Shelley, issuing from it more cautious, more sober, — one is tempted to say, more prosaic. By disposition and training, Shelley was rather Hellenic, Sidney rather Roman. Sidney followed of preference the matter-of-fact Aristotle, while Shelley was more admiringly attached to the ardent and soaring Plato, —

not the Plato of the *Republic*, but him of the *Ion* and the *Symposium*. In considering the ancient drama, Shelley has his eye upon the Athenians, Sidney upon Seneca and Plautus. His acquaintance with Greek literature enabled Shelley to assume toward Roman poetry the attitude of a stern but upright judge; this is shown as well in his appreciation of Lucretius as in his estimate of the general literary inferiority of the Romans, and in his censure of the Alexandrianism upon which no small part of the Latin poetry was nourished.

The moral instruction which poetry should impart appears, according to Sidney, to be, as it were, mechanically suspended in the liquid mass of poetry; according to Sidney, the bubbling wellspring of poetry is highly charged with secret medicinal virtue, which renders still more agreeable the medium by which it is conveyed. The one seeks to disguise a wholesome bitterness; the other is conscious of nothing but an exhilarating and healthful potency. Sidney, in his utilitarian vein, can condescend to speak of the mnemonic value of verse. He presents himself before us as an advocate holding a brief for a discredited client, and seeking to convince by any fair means, even to the sacrifice of the defendant's dignity. His eloquence is forensic and practical, like the literary genius of Rome. It deals with the tangible, the ponderable; with it he descends into the arena in order to conquer. Once there, if his adversary's armor resist the keen thrust of his sword, he is willing, like a Homeric hero, to cast about for some convenient boulder with which to crush him. Shelley, on the other hand, disdains to leave the empyrean. Thence if he hurl a missile, it shall be the bolt of Jove, which dazzles while it smites. To his glance the farthest horizons are simultaneously disclosed. Accordingly, he recognizes the identity of poetry with invention; with every species of fine art; with the prescience of great lawgivers; with an intuitional philosophy; with vision which, in the poverty of language, we call prophetic, but which is really timeless, affirmatory of an eternal Now.

Shelley's historical perspective is larger and juster than Sidney's ; he sees the ages unroll the panoramic destinies of the race, and marks the elements of renewal and decay. He gazes critically at the past, and hopefully into the future. Sidney could not see a decade in advance, could not even discern the youthful Shakespeare ; Shelley virtually foresaw the whole transcendental movement in England and America, with the train of beneficial effects by which it was to be accompanied. In a word and a figure, if Sidney is mounted on a strong and active steed, it is still of mortal strain, while Shelley is aloft on Pegasus, and scarcely condescends to touch the ground in his airy flight.

3. THE PROVINCES OF INSPIRATION AND OF LABOR.

In one point of the highest importance Shelley has perhaps expressed himself too strongly. Speaking of the impotence of the will in the production of poetry, he explains (p. 39) : " I appeal to the greatest poets of the present day whether it is not an error to assert that the finest passages of poetry are produced by labor and study. The toil and the delay recommended by critics can be justly interpreted to mean no more than a careful observation of the inspired moments, and an artificial connection of the spaces between their suggestions by the intertexture of conventional expressions."

The decision in this matter is one that can be given by none so well as by the poets themselves. What testimony is borne by the ancients, and what by the moderns? If it were possible to compare the utterances of men so various as Pindar, Horace, Dante, Milton, Goethe, Schiller, Burns, and Shelley himself — Shelley the artist rather than Shelley the theorist — it would seem that the question might be settled.

Pindar is usually regarded as the type of the fiery and

impassioned poet. In certain of his odes he characterizes his own processes. Do these exclude labor and study? According to that most accomplished and poetic of his editors, Professor Gildersleeve, it is quite otherwise (p. xxxvi) : " Of the richness of his workmanship none is better aware than he. The work of the poet is a Dædalian work, and the sinuous folds are wrought with rare skill (O. 1, 105), the art of art is selection and adornment, the production of a rich and compassed surface (P. 9, 83). ˙ The splendor of the Goddesses of Triumphal Song irradiates him (P. 9, 97), and he is a leader in the skill of poesy, which to him is by eminence wisdom (σοφία), wisdom in the art of the theme, and in the art of the treatment." And again (p. xliii) : " Pindar is a jeweller, his material gold and ivory, and his chryselephantine work challenges the scrutiny of the microscope, invites the study that wearies not day or night in exploring the recesses in which the artist has held his art sequestered — invites the study and rewards it."

To the same effect is the judgment of Croiset, the author of a fascinating book entitled *La Poésie de Pindare* (pp. 153-5): " From what precedes it will be sufficiently clear that we should be forming a totally false notion of Greek lyric poetry, if, in conformity with certain modern prepossessions, we supposed it to be the product of unreasoning impulse and blind inspiration. Nothing is less artless, in one way, than the fine frenzy of the Greek lyric. In these show-pieces of his art, the poet has but a general and remote interest in the things of which he is discoursing. It is solely by means of the imagination, and in a manner wholly artificial, that he succeeds in arousing his own emotional activity. Friendship, gratitude for open-handed hospitality, even piety in its stated and formal manifestations, are not sentiments which can ravish the poet out of his self-possession ; and we can attribute still less influence to the stipulated fee, often the immediate cause of his strains. There are a thousand proprieties for him to observe. He must possess tact and pliancy of spirit which shall be equal to every occasion. Nothing is more difficult than to eulogize gracefully, — and precisely in this the whole art of the lyric poet consists. Whether gods or men form his subject, praise is his exclusive concern. Hence it is deep and continuous reflection, not ecstasy of any sort, which will conduct him to his goal. If ecstasy has any share in the production, it is chiefly in the final working up of his materials, after art and learning have foreseen everything, calculated and disposed everything, with reference to the effect intended.

" To all this the lyric poets paid full heed. In the preceding pages we have already passed in review a considerable number of Pindar's verses which contain allusions to laws by which he felt himself bound. At other times he pretends to lose his way, — then checks and corrects himself, and leads his chariot back again into the right road, and by so doing furnishes the proof that even his poetic rapture never ceases to keep watch over itself. The lyric poets often allude to reefs on which they must beware of shattering their barks. Now the danger is one of excessive length, now of a superfluity of praise, again of triteness or monotony. Consummate skill is necessary in order to avoid these perils. Nothing is less like a wild and headlong career than this circumspect advance, so mindful of all its steps in the midst of its superb dignity and magnificent speed. The lyric poet calls himself a cunning workman, a craft-master, for so we may translate the Greek words σοφός and σοφιστής which Pindar employs. He speaks of his talent as readily as of his Muse. He is fully conscious of his art and prides himself upon it. It is not through some chance inspiration that he brings to light such marvels; it is through a science which is perfectly master of itself, through an art which adds to the gifts of the Graces and the Muses that which is no less necessary, experience and craftsmanship. The poet's inspiration is subject to laws, to fixed rules. These he must know and to these he must submit."

Of Horace, generally esteemed the calmer and saner mind, the dictum is well-known (*Art of Poetry*, 408–411) : " Whether by genius or by art an excellent poem is produced, has often been the question ; but I do not see what can be done by study without a rich vein of intellect, nor by genius when uncultivated ; so true is it that either requires the help of either, and that the two combine in friendly union."

Dante has been quoted in the note to the passage. Milton, though in a quite different form of words, virtually echoes the Horatian sentiment (*Reason of Church Government*) : " I began thus far to assent both to them and divers of my friends here at home, and not less to an inward prompting which now grew daily upon me, that by labor and intense study, which I take to be my portion in this life, joined with the strong propensity of nature, I might perhaps leave something so written to aftertimes, as they should not willingly let it die. . . . I applied myself to that resolution which Ariosto followed against the persuasions of Bembo, to fix all the industry and art I could unite to the adorning of my native tongue. . . . Nor to be obtained by the invocation of Dame Memory and her siren daughters, but by devout prayer to that eternal Spirit who can enrich with all utterance and knowledge, and sends out his seraphim with the hallowed fire of his altar, to touch and purify the lips of whom he pleases. To this must be added industrious and select reading, steady observation, insight into all seemly and generous arts and affairs."

Goethe might be quoted in favor of the extreme view, and might even be thought to go further than Shelley himself (*Eckermann*, March 11, 1828) : " No productiveness of the highest kind, no remarkable discovery, no great thought which bears fruit and has results, is in the power of any one ;

such things are elevated above all earthly control. Man must consider them as an unexpected gift from above, as the pure efflux of divine grace which he must receive and venerate with joyful thanks. They are akin to the δαίμον, or genius of life, which does with him what it pleases, and to which he unconsciously resigns himself, whilst he believes he is acting from his own impulse. In such cases, man may best be considered as an instrument in the higher government of the world, as a vessel found worthy for the reception of a divine influence. I say this while I consider how often a single thought has given a different form to whole centuries; and how individual men have, by their expressions, imprinted a stamp upon their age, which has remained uneffaced, and has operated beneficially upon many succeeding generations." But against this must be alleged evidence tending to correct such an impression (Letter to Schiller, April 19, 1797) : "Some verses in Homer, which are pronounced to be certainly not genuine and quite new, are of the same kind as some which I myself interpolated into my poem, after it was finished, in order to make the whole clearer and more intelligible, and to prepare betimes future events. I am very curious to see what I shall be inclined to add to or take from my poem, when I shall have got through with my present studies."

Of Schiller, Goethe says (*Eckermann*, Nov. 14, 1823) : "Schiller produced nothing instinctively or unconsciously ; he must reflect upon every step ; therefore he always wished to talk over his literary plans, and has conversed with me about all his later works, piece by piece, as he was writing them." And Schiller describes his own procedure when engaged upon the Song of the Bell (Letter to Goethe, July 7, 1797) : "I have now gone to work at my bell-founder's song, and since yesterday I have been studying in Kruenitz's Encyclopædia, out of which I get a great deal of profit. This poem I have much at heart, but it will cost me several

weeks, because I need for it so many varieties of moods,
and there is a great bulk to be worked up."

In a bookseller's catalogue of manuscripts I find a quotation in point from an alleged autograph letter of Burns, said
to bear date of Jan. 22, 1788, which, however, does not
appear in any of the published collections in that place.
The quotation is : "I have no great faith in the boasted
pretensions to intuitive propriety and unlabored elegance.
The rough material of fine writing is certainly the gift of
genius. But I as firmly believe that the workmanship is the
united effort of pains, attention, and repeated trial."

The principle of composition, as distinguished from direct
inspiration, was certainly recognized by Shelley, for he avows
that he acted upon it in the writing of *Adonais* (Letter to
Mr. and Mrs. Gisborne, June 5, 1821) : "I have been engaged these last days in composing a poem on the death of
Keats, which will shortly be finished. . . . It is a highly
wrought *piece of art*, and perhaps better, in point of composition, than anything I have written."

Perhaps as good a summary as is required may be found
in Saintsbury's note on the passage which has called forth
this comment (*Specimens of English Prose*, p. 346) : "There
is an obvious fallacy here. The finest passages are not origi-
nally inspired by labor and study, but in their finest shape
they are the result of labor and study spent on the immediate result of inspiration."

A DEFENSE OF POETRY.

ACCORDING to one mode of regarding those two
classes of mental action which are called reason
and imagination, the former may be considered as
mind contemplating the relations borne by one
thought to another, however produced, and the 5
latter as mind acting upon those thoughts so as
to color them with its own light, and composing
from them, as from elements, other thoughts, each
containing within itself the principle of its own
integrity. The one is the τὸ ποιεῖν, or the princi- 10
ple of synthesis, and has for its object those forms
which are common to universal nature and existence itself; the other is the τὸ λογίζειν, or principle
of analysis, and its action regards the relations of
things simply as relations; considering thoughts 15
not in their integral unity, but as the algebraical
representations which conduct to certain general
results. Reason is the enumeration of quantities
already known; imagination is the perception of
the value of those quantities, both separately and 20
as a whole. Reason respects the differences, and
imagination the similitudes of things. Reason is
to imagination as the instrument to the agent, as
the body to the spirit, as the shadow to the substance. 25

Poetry, in a general sense, may be defined to be 'the expression of the imagination'; and poetry is connate with the origin of man. Man is an instrument over which a series of external and internal impressions are driven, like the alternations of an ever-changing wind over an Æolian lyre, which move it by their motion to ever-changing melody. But there is a principle within the human being, and perhaps within all sentient beings, which acts otherwise than in a lyre, and produces not melody alone, but harmony, by an internal adjustment of the sounds and motions thus excited to the impressions which excite them. It is as if the lyre could accommodate its chords to the motions of that which strikes them, in a determined proportion of sound; even as the musician can accommodate his voice to the sound of the lyre. A child at play by itself will express its delight by its voice and motions; and every inflection of tone and every gesture will bear exact relation to a corresponding antitype in the pleasurable impressions which awakened it; it will be the reflected image of that impression; and as the lyre trembles and sounds after the wind has died away, so the child seeks, by prolonging in its voice and motions the duration of the effect, to prolong also a consciousness of the cause. In relation to the objects which delight a child, these expressions are what poetry is to higher objects. The savage (for the savage is to ages what the child is to years) expresses the emotions produced in him by surrounding objects in a similar manner; and language and gesture, together with plastic or pictorial imitation, become the image of the combined effect of those objects and his apprehension of them. Man in society, with all his passions and his pleasures, next becomes the object of the passions and pleasures of man ; an additional class of emotions produces an 5 augmented treasure of expression ; and language, gesture, and the imitative arts, become at once the representation and the medium, the pencil and the picture, the chisel and the statue, the chord and the harmony. The social sympathies, or those 10 laws from which, as from its elements, society results, begin to develop themselves from the moment that two human beings co-exist ; the future is contained within the present as the plant within the seed ; and equality, diversity, unity, 15 contrast, mutual dependence, become the principles alone capable of affording the motives according to which the will of a social being is determined to action, inasmuch as he is social ; and constitute pleasure in sensation, virtue in sen- 20 timent, beauty in art, truth in reasoning, and love in the intercourse of kind. Hence men, even in the infancy of society, observe a certain order in their words and actions, distinct from that of the objects and the impressions represented by them, 25 all expression being subject to the laws of that from which it proceeds. But let us dismiss those more general considerations which might involve an inquiry into the principles of society itself, and restrict our view to the manner in which the imag- 30 ination is expressed upon its forms.

In the youth of the world, men dance and sing and imitate natural objects, observing in these

actions, as in all others, a certain rhythm or order.
And, although all men observe a similar, they
observe not the same order in the motions of the
dance, in the melody of the song, in the combina-
5 tions of language, in the series of their imitations
of natural objects. For there is a certain order
or rhythm belonging to each of these classes of
mimetic representation, from which the hearer and
the spectator receive an intenser and purer pleas-
10 ure than from any other; the sense of an approximation to this order has been called taste by
modern writers. Every man, in the infancy of art,
observes an order which approximates more or less
closely to that from which this highest delight
15 results; but the diversity is not sufficiently marked
as that its gradations should be sensible, except in
those instances where the predominance of this
faculty of approximation to the beautiful (for so
we may be permitted to name the relation between
20 this highest pleasure and its cause) is very great.
Those in whom it exists to excess are poets, in the
most universal sense of the word; and the pleasure
resulting from the manner in which they express
the influence of society or nature upon their own
25 minds, communicates itself to others, and gathers
a sort of reduplication from the community.
Their language is vitally metaphorical; that is, it
marks the before unapprehended relations of things
and perpetuates their apprehension, until words,
30 which represent them, become, through time, signs
for portions or classes of thought instead of pic-
tures of integral thoughts; and then, if no new
poets should arise to create afresh the associations

which have been thus disorganized, language will
be dead to all the nobler purposes of human intercourse. These similitudes or relations are finely
said by Lord Bacon to be "the same footsteps of
nature impressed upon the various subjects of the 5
world"—and he considers the faculty which per-
ceives them as the storehouse of axioms common
to all knowledge. In the infancy of society every
author is necessarily a poet, because language
itself is poetry; and to be a poet is to apprehend 10
the true and the beautiful, in a word, the good
which exists in the relation subsisting, first between existence and perception, and secondly between perception and expression. Every original
language near to its source is in itself the chaos of 15
a cyclic poem; the copiousness of lexicography
and the distinctions of grammar are the works of
a later age, and are merely the catalogue and the
forms of the creations of poetry.

But poets, or those who imagine and express 20
this indestructible order, are not only the authors
of language and of music, of the dance, and architecture, and statuary, and painting: they are the
institutors of laws, and the founders of civil society, and the inventors of the arts of life, and the 25
teachers who draw into a certain propinquity with
the beautiful and the true that partial apprehension of the agencies of the invisible world which
is called religion. Hence all original religions are
allegorical, or susceptible of allegory, and, like 30
Janus, have a double face of false and true. Poets,
according to the circumstances of the age and
nation in which they appeared, were called, in the

earlier epochs of the world, legislators or prophets;
a poet essentially comprises and unites both these
characters.   For he not only beholds intensely
the present as it is, and discovers those laws accord-
5 ing to which present things ought to be ordered,
but he beholds the future in the present, and his
thoughts are the germs of the flower and the fruit
of latest time.   Not that I assert poets to be
prophets in the gross sense of the word, or that
10 they can foretell the form as surely as they fore-
know the spirit of events; such is the pretence of
superstition, which would make poetry an attribute
of prophecy, rather than prophecy an attribute of
poetry.   A poet participates in the eternal, the
15 infinite, and the one; as far as relates to his conceptions, time and place and number are not.   The
grammatical forms which express the moods of
time, and the difference of persons, and the distinction of place, are convertible with respect to
20 the highest poetry without injuring it as poetry;
and the choruses of Æschylus, and the Book of
Job, and Dante's Paradise, would afford, more than
any other writings, examples of this fact, if the
limits of this essay did not forbid citation.   The
25 creations of music, sculpture, and painting are
illustrations still more decisive.

Language, color, form, and religious and civil
habits of action, are all the instruments and materials of poetry; they may be called poetry by that
30 figure of speech which considers the effect as a
synonym of the cause.   But poetry in a more
restricted sense expresses those arrangements of
language, and especially metrical language, which

are created by that imperial faculty whose throne
is curtained within the invisible nature of man.
And this springs from the nature itself of language, which is a more direct representation of the
actions and passions of our internal being, and is 5
susceptible of more various and delicate combinations, than color, form, or motion, and is more plastic and obedient to the control of that faculty of
which it is the creation. For language is arbitra-
rily produced by the imagination, and has relation 10
to thoughts alone; but all other materials, instruments, and conditions of art have relations among
each other, which limit and interpose between conception and expression. The former is as a mirror
which reflects, the latter as a cloud which enfeebles, 15
the light of which both are mediums of communication. Hence the fame of sculptors, painters,
and musicians, although the intrinsic powers of the
great masters of these arts may yield in no degree
to that of those who have employed language as 20
the hieroglyphic of their thoughts, has never
equalled that of poets in the restricted sense of
the term; as two performers of equal skill will
produce unequal effects from a guitar and a harp.
The fame of legislators and founders of religions, 25
so long as their institutions last, alone seems to
exceed that of poets in the restricted sense; but
it can scarcely be a question, whether, if we deduct
the celebrity which their flattery of the gross
opinions of the vulgar usually conciliates, together 30
with that which belonged to them in their higher
character of poets, any excess will remain.

We have thus circumscribed the word poetry

within the limits of that art which is the most familiar and the most perfect expression of the faculty itself. It is necessary, however, to make the circle still narrower, and to determine the dis-
5 tinction between measured and unmeasured language; for the popular division into prose and verse is inadmissible in accurate philosophy.

Sounds as well as thoughts have relation both between each other and towards that which they
10 represent, and a perception of the order of those relations has always been found connected with a perception of the order of the relations of thoughts. Hence the language of poets has ever affected a sort of uniform and harmonious recurrence of
15 sound, without which it were not poetry, and which is scarcely less indispensable to the communication of its influence than the words themselves without reference to that peculiar order. Hence the vanity of translation; it were as wise
20 to cast a violet into a crucible that you might discover the formal principles of its color and odor, as seek to transfuse from one language into another the creations of a poet. The plant must spring again from its seed, or it will bear no flower — and
25 this is the burthen of the curse of Babel.

An observation of the regular mode of the recurrence of harmony in the language of poetical minds, together with its relation to music, produced metre, or a certain system of traditional forms of
30 harmony and language. Yet it is by no means essential that a poet should accommodate his language to this traditional form, so that the harmony, which is its spirit, be observed. The practice is

indeed convenient and popular, and to be preferred
especially in such composition as includes much
action ; but every great poet must inevitably inno-
vate upon the example of his predecessors in the
exact structure of his peculiar versification. The 5
distinction between poets and prose writers is a
vulgar error. The distinction between philosophers and poets has been anticipated. Plato was
essentially a poet — the truth and splendor of his
imagery, and the melody of his language, are the 10
most intense that it is possible to conceive. He
rejected the harmony of the epic, dramatic, and
lyrical forms, because he sought to kindle a harmony in thoughts divested of shape and action,
and he forbore to invent any regular plan of rhythm 15
which would include, under determinate forms, the
varied pauses of his style. Cicero sought to imitate the cadence of his periods, but with little success. Lord Bacon was a poet. His language has
a sweet and majestic rhythm which satisfies the 20
sense, no less than the almost superhuman wisdom
of his philosophy satisfies the intellect ; it is a
strain which distends and then bursts the circumference of the reader's mind, and pours itself forth
together with it into the universal element with 25
which it has perpetual sympathy. All the authors
of revolutions in opinion are not only necessarily
poets as they are inventors, nor even as their words
unveil the permanent analogy of things by images
which participate in the life of truth ; but as their 30
periods are harmonious and rhythmical, and contain
in themselves the elements of verse; being the
echo of the eternal music. Nor are those supreme

poets, who have employed traditional forms of rhythm on account of the form and action of their subjects, less capable of perceiving and teaching the truth of things, than those who have omitted 5 that form. Shakespeare, Dante, and Milton (to confine ourselves to modern writers) are philosophers of the very loftiest power.

A poem is the very image of life expressed in its eternal truth. There is this difference between a 10 story and a poem, that a story is a catalogue of detached facts, which have no other connection than time, place, circumstance, cause and effect; the other is the creation of actions according to the unchangeable forms of human nature, as exist-15 ing in the mind of the creator, which is itself the image of all other minds. The one is partial, and applies only to a definite period of time, and a certain combination of events which can never again recur; the other is universal, and contains within 20 itself the germ of a relation to whatever motives or actions have place in the possible varieties of human nature. Time, which destroys the beauty and the use of the story of particular facts, stripped of the poetry which should invest them, 25 augments that of poetry, and for ever develops new and wonderful applications of the eternal truth which it contains. Hence epitomes have been called the moths of just history; they eat out the poetry of it. A story of particular facts is as a 30 mirror which obscures and distorts that which should be beautiful; poetry is a mirror which makes beautiful that which is distorted.

The parts of a composition may be poetical,

without the composition as a whole being a poem.
A single sentence may be considered as a whole,
though it may be found in the midst of a series of
unassimilated portions; a single word even may
be a spark of inextinguishable thought. And thus
all the great historians, Herodotus, Plutarch, Livy,
were poets; and although the plan of these writers,
especially that of Livy, restrained them from
developing this faculty in its highest degree, they
made copious and ample amends for their subjec- 10
tion, by filling all the interstices of their subjects
with living images.

Having determined what is poetry, and who are
poets, let us proceed to estimate its effects upon
society. 15

Poetry is ever accompanied with pleasure : all
spirits on which it falls open themselves to receive
the wisdom which is mingled with its delight. In
the infancy of the world, neither poets themselves
nor their auditors are fully aware of the excellency 20
of poetry, for it acts in a divine and unapprehended manner, beyond and above consciousness;
and it is reserved for future generations to contemplate and measure the mighty cause and effect in
all the strength and splendor of their union. Even 25
in modern times, no living poet ever arrived at the
fulness of his fame; the jury which sits in judgment upon a poet, belonging as he does to all time,
must be composed of his peers; it must be impanelled by Time from the selectest of the wise of 30
many generations. A poet is a nightingale, who
sits in darkness and sings to cheer its own solitude
with sweet sounds; his auditors are as men en-

tranced by the melody of an unseen musician, who
feel that they are moved and softened, yet know
not whence or why. The poems of Homer and
his contemporaries were the delight of infant
5 Greece; they were the elements of that social system which is the column upon which all succeeding
civilization has reposed. Homer embodied the
ideal perfection of his age in human character;
nor can we doubt that those who read his verses
10 were awakened to an ambition of becoming like
to Achilles, Hector, and Ulysses; the truth and
beauty of friendship, patriotism, and persevering
devotion to an object, were unveiled to their depths
in these immortal creations; the sentiments of the
15 auditors must have been refined and enlarged by a
sympathy with such great and lovely impersonations, until from admiring they imitated, and from
imitation they identified themselves with the objects
of their admiration. Nor let it be objected that
20 these characters are remote from moral perfection,
and that they are by no means to be considered as
edifying patterns for general imitation. Every
epoch, under names more or less specious, has
deified its peculiar errors; Revenge is the naked
25 idol of the worship of a semi-barbarous age; and
Self-deceit is the veiled image of unknown evil,
before which luxury and satiety lie prostrate. But
a poet considers the vices of his contemporaries as
the temporary dress in which his creations must be
30 arrayed, and which cover without concealing the
eternal proportions of their beauty. An epic or
dramatic personage is understood to wear them
around his soul, as he may the ancient armor or

modern uniform around his body; whilst it is easy
to conceive a dress more graceful than either. The
beauty of the internal nature can not be so far concealed by its accidental vesture, but that the spirit
of its form shall communicate itself to the very 5
disguise, and indicate the shape it hides from the
manner in which it is worn. A majestic form and
graceful motions will express themselves through
the most barbarous and tasteless costume. Few
poets of the highest class have chosen to exhibit 10
the beauty of their conceptions in its naked truth
and splendor ; and it is doubtful whether the alloy
of costume, habit, etc., be not necessary to temper this planetary music for mortal ears.

The whole objection, however, of the immorality 15
of poetry rests upon a misconception of the manner in which poetry acts to produce the moral
improvement of man. Ethical science arranges
the elements which poetry has created, and pro-
pounds schemes and proposes examples of civil 20
and domestic life ; nor is it for want of admirable
doctrines that men hate, and despise, and censure,
and deceive, and subjugate one another. But poetry acts in another and diviner manner. It awakens
and enlarges the mind itself by rendering it the 25
receptacle of a thousand unapprehended combinations of thought. Poetry lifts the veil from the
hidden beauty of the world, and makes familiar
objects be as if they were not familiar ; it reproduces all that it represents, and the impersonations 30
clothed in its Elysian light stand thenceforward in
the minds of those who have once contemplated
them, as memorials of that gentle and exalted con-

tent which extends itself over all thoughts and actions with which it co-exists. The great secret of morals is love; or a going out of our own nature, and an identification of ourselves with the beauti-
5 ful which exists in thought, action, or person, not our own. A man, to be greatly good, must imagine intensely and comprehensively; he must put himself in the place of another and of many others; the pains and pleasures of his species must
10 become his own. The great instrument of moral good is the imagination; and poetry administers to the effect by acting upon the cause. Poetry enlarges the circumference of the imagination by replenishing it with thoughts of ever new delight,
15 which have the power of attracting and assimilating to their own nature all other thoughts, and which form new intervals and interstices whose void for ever craves fresh food. Poetry strengthens the faculty which is the organ of the moral nature
20 of man, in the same manner as exercise strengthens a limb. A poet therefore would do ill to embody his own conceptions of right and wrong, which are usually those of his place and time, in his poetical creations, which participate in neither.
25 By this assumption of the inferior office of interpreting the effect, in which perhaps after all he might acquit himself but imperfectly, he would resign a glory in the participation of the cause. There was little danger that Homer, or any of the
30 eternal poets, should have so far misunderstood themselves as to have abdicated this throne of their widest dominion. Those in whom the poetical faculty, though great, is less intense, as Euri-

pides, Lucan, Tasso, Spenser, have frequently
affected a moral aim, and the effect of their poetry
is diminished in exact proportion to the degree in
which they compel us to advert to this purpose.

Homer and the cyclic poets were followed at a 5
certain interval by the dramatic and lyrical poets of
Athens, who flourished contemporaneously with
all that is most perfect in the kindred expressions
of the poetical faculty: architecture, painting, music,
the dance, sculpture, philosophy, and we may add, 10
the forms of civil life. For although the scheme
of Athenian society was deformed by many imper-
fections which the poetry existing in chivalry and
Christianity has erased from the habits and institutions of modern Europe; yet never at any other 15
period has so much energy, beauty, and virtue
been developed; never was blind strength and
stubborn form so disciplined and rendered subject
to the will of man, or that will less repugnant to
the dictates of the beautiful and the true, as during 20
the century which preceded the death of Socrates.
Of no other epoch in the history of our species
have we records and fragments stamped so visibly
with the image of the divinity in man. But it is
poetry alone, in form, in action, and in language, 25
which has rendered this epoch memorable above all
others, and the storehouse of examples to everlasting time. For written poetry existed at that epoch
simultaneously with the other arts, and it is an idle
inquiry to demand which gave and which received 30
the light, which all, as from a common focus, have
scattered over the darkest periods of succeeding
time. We know no more of cause and effect than

a constant conjunction of events; poetry is ever found to co-exist with whatever other arts contribute to the happiness and perfection of man. I appeal to what has already been established to dis-
5 tinguish between the cause and the effect.

It was at the period here adverted to that the drama had its birth; and however a succeeding writer may have equalled or surpassed those few great specimens of the Athenian drama which have
10 been preserved to us, it is indisputable that the art itself never was understood or practised according to the true philosophy of it, as at Athens. For the Athenians employed language, action, music, painting, the dance, and religious institution, to
15 produce a common effect in the representation of the highest idealisms of passion and of power; each division in the art was made perfect in its kind by artists of the most consummate skill, and was disciplined into a beautiful proportion and
20 unity one towards the other. On the modern stage a few only of the elements capable of expressing the image of the poet's conception are employed at once. We have tragedy without music and dancing, and music and dancing without the highest
25 impersonations of which they are the fit accompaniment, and both without religion and solemnity. Religious institution has indeed been usually banished from the stage. Our system of divesting the actor's face of a mask, on which the many
30 expressions appropriated to his dramatic character might be moulded into one permanent and unchanging expression, is favorable only to a partial and inharmonious effect; it is fit for nothing but a

monologue, where all the attention may be directed
to some great master of ideal mimicry. The modern practice of blending comedy with tragedy,
though liable to great abuse in point of practice, is
undoubtedly an extension of the dramatic circle; 5
but the comedy should be as in King Lear, universal, ideal, and sublime. It is perhaps the intervention of this principle which determines the balance
in favor of King Lear against the Œdipus Tyran-
nus or the Agamemnon, or, if you will, the trilogies 10
with which they are connected; unless the intense
power of the choral poetry, especially that of the
latter, should be considered as restoring the equilib-
rium. King Lear, if it can sustain this comparison,
may be judged to be the most perfect specimen of 15
the dramatic art existing in the world, in spite of
the narrow conditions to which the poet was subjected by the ignorance of the philosophy of the
drama which has prevailed in modern Europe.
Calderon, in his religious Autos, has attempted to 20
fulfil some of the high conditions of dramatic representation neglected by Shakespeare; such as the
establishing a relation between the drama and
religion, and the accommodating them to music
and dancing; but he omits the observation of con- 25
ditions still more important, and more is lost than
gained by the substitution of the rigidly-defined
and ever-repeated idealisms of a distorted superstition for the living impersonations of the truth of
human passion. 30

But I digress. — The connection of scenic exhi-
bitions with the improvement or corruption of the
manners of men has been universally recognized;

in other words, the presence or absence of poetry
in its most perfect and universal form has been
found to be connected with good and evil in conduct or habit. The corruption which has been
5 imputed to the drama as an effect begins when
the poetry employed in its constitution ends; I
appeal to the history of manners whether the
periods of the growth of the one and the decline
of the other have not corresponded with an exact-
10 ness equal to any example of moral cause and
effect.

The drama at Athens, or wheresoever else it
may have approached to its perfection, ever co-
existed with the moral and intellectual greatness of
15 the age. The tragedies of the Athenian poets are
as mirrors in which the spectator beholds himself,
under a thin disguise of circumstance, stripped of all
but that ideal perfection and energy which every
one feels to be the internal type of all that he
20 loves, admires, and would become. The imagination is enlarged by a sympathy with pains and
passions so mighty, that they distend in their
conception the capacity of that by which they are
conceived ; the good affections are strengthened by
25 pity, indignation, terror and sorrow, and an exalted
calm is prolonged from the satiety of this high
exercise of them into the tumult of familiar life ;
even crime is disarmed of half its horror and all
its contagion by being represented as the fatal con-
30 sequence of the unfathomable agencies of nature ;
error is thus divested of its wilfulness ; men can
no longer cherish it as the creation of their choice.
In the drama of the highest order there is little food

for censure or hatred; it teaches rather self-knowledge and self-respect. Neither the eye nor the
mind can see itself, unless reflected upon that
which it resembles. The drama, so long as it
continues to express poetry, is a prismatic and 5
many-sided mirror, which collects the brightest
rays of human nature and divides and reproduces
them from the simplicity of their elementary
forms, and touches them with majesty and beauty,
and multiplies all that it reflects, and endows it 10
with the power of propagating its like wherever it
may fall.

But in periods of the decay of social life, the
drama sympathizes with that decay. Tragedy becomes a cold imitation of the forms of the great 15
masterpieces of antiquity, divested of all harmonious accompaniment of the kindred arts; and often
the very form misunderstood, or a weak attempt to
teach certain doctrines which the writer considers
as moral truths, and which are usually no more 20
than specious flatteries of some gross vice or weak-
ness with which the author, in common with his
auditors, are infected. Hence what has been called
the classical and domestic drama. Addison's
'Cato' is a specimen of the one; and would it 25
were not superfluous to cite examples of the other!
To such purposes poetry cannot be made subser-
vient. Poetry is a sword of lightning, ever un-
sheathed, which consumes the scabbard that would
contain it. And hence we observe that all dramatic 30
writings of this nature are unimaginative in a sin-
gular degree; they affect sentiment and passion,
which, divested of imagination, are other names

for caprice and appetite. The period in our own
history of the grossest degradation of the drama
is the reign of Charles II., when all forms in which
poetry had been accustomed to be expressed be-
5 came hymns to the triumph of kingly power over
liberty and virtue. Milton stood alone, illuminat-
ing an age unworthy of him. At such periods
the calculating principle pervades all the forms of
dramatic exhibition, and poetry ceases to be
10 expressed upon them. Comedy loses its ideal universality; wit succeeds to humor; we laugh from
self-complacency and triumph, instead of pleasure;
malignity, sarcasm, and contempt succeed to sympathetic merriment; we hardly laugh, but we smile.
15 Obscenity, which is ever blasphemy against the
divine beauty in life, becomes, from the very veil
which it assumes, more active if less disgusting;
it is a monster for which the corruption of society
for ever brings forth new food, which it devours in
20 secret.

The drama being that form under which a greater
number of modes of expression of poetry are susceptible of being combined than any other, the
connection of poetry and social good is more
25 observable in the drama than in whatever other
form. And it is indisputable that the highest perfection of human society has ever corresponded
with the highest dramatic excellence; and that the
corruption or the extinction of the drama in a
30 nation where it has once flourished, is a mark of a
corruption of manners, and an extinction of the
energies which sustain the soul of social life. But,
as Machiavelli says of political institutions, that

life may be preserved and renewed, if men should
arise capable of bringing back the drama to its
principles. And this is true with respect to poetry
in its most extended sense ; all language, institution
and form, require not only to be produced but to be 5
sustained ; the office and character of a poet participates in the divine nature as regards providence,
no less than as regards creation.

Civil war, the spoils of Asia, and the fatal predominance first of the Macedonian, and then of 10
the Roman arms, were so many symbols of the
extinction or suspension of the creative faculty in
Greece. The bucolic writers, who found patronage
under the lettered tyrants of Sicily and Egypt,
were the latest representatives of its most glorious 15
reign. Their poetry is intensely melodious ; like
the odor of the tuberose, it overcomes and sickens
the spirit with excess of sweetness ; whilst the
poetry of the preceding age was as a meadow-gale
of June, which mingles the fragrance of all the 20
flowers of the field, and adds a quickening and
harmonizing spirit of its own which endows the
sense with a power of sustaining its extreme
delight. The bucolic and erotic delicacy in written
poetry is correlative with that softness in statuary, 25
music, and the kindred arts, and even in manners
and institutions, which distinguished the epoch to
which I now refer. Nor is it the poetical faculty
itself, or any misapplication of it, to which this
want of harmony is to be imputed. An equal sen- 30
sibility to the influence of the senses and the affections is to be found in the writings of Homer and
Sophocles ; the former, especially, has clothed sen-

sual and pathetic images with irresistible attrac-
tions. Their superiority over these succeeding
writers consists in the presence of those thoughts
which belong to the inner faculties of our nature,
5 not in the absence of those which are connected
with the external; their incomparable perfection
consists in a harmony of the union of all. It is
not what the erotic poets have, but what they have
not, in which their imperfection consists. It is not
10 inasmuch as they were poets, but inasmuch as they
were not poets, that they can be considered with
any plausibility as connected with the corruption
of their age. Had that corruption availed so as to
extinguish in them the sensibility to pleasure, pas-
15 sion, and natural scenery which is imputed to
them as an imperfection, the last triumph of evil
would have been achieved. For the end of social
corruption is to destroy all sensibility to pleasure;
and therefore it is corruption. It begins at the
20 imagination and the intellect as at the core, and
distributes itself thence as a paralyzing venom
through the affections into the very appetites,
until all become a torpid mass in which hardly
sense survives. At the approach of such a period,
25 poetry ever addresses itself to those faculties which
are the last to be destroyed, and its voice is heard,
like the footsteps of Astræa, departing from the
world. Poetry ever communicates all the pleasure
which men are capable of receiving; it is ever still
30 the light of life, the source of whatever of beautiful or generous or true can have place in an evil
time. It will readily be confessed that those
among the luxurious citizens of Syracuse and

Alexandria who were delighted with the poems of
Theocritus were less cold, cruel, and sensual than
the remnant of their tribe. But corruption must
utterly have destroyed the fabric of human society
before poetry can ever cease. The sacred links of 5
that chain have never been entirely disjoined,
which descending through the minds of many men
is attached to those great minds, whence as from
a magnet the invisible effluence is sent forth, which
at once connects, animates, and sustains the life of 10
all. It is the faculty which contains within itself
the seeds at once of its own and of social renova-
tion. And let us not circumscribe the effects of
the bucolic and erotic poetry within the limits of
the sensibility of those to whom it was addressed. 15
They may have perceived the beauty of those
immortal compositions, simply as fragments and
isolated portions ; those who are more finely organized, or born in a happier age, may recognize them
as episodes to that great poem, which all poets, 20
like the co-operating thoughts of one great mind,
have built up since the beginning of the world.

The same revolution within a narrower sphere
had place in ancient Rome ; but the actions and
forms of its social life never seem to have been 25
perfectly saturated with the poetical element. The
Romans appear to have considered the Greeks as
the selectest treasuries of the selectest forms of
manners and of nature, and to have abstained from
creating in measured language, sculpture, music, 30
or architecture, any thing which might bear a particular relation to their own condition, whilst it
should bear a general one to the universal consti-

tution of the world.   But we judge from partial
evidence, and we judge perhaps partially.   Ennius,
Varro, Pacuvius, and Accius, all great poets, have
been lost.   Lucretius is in the highest, and Virgil
5 in a very high sense, a creator.   The chosen delicacy of expressions of the latter are as a mist of
light which conceal from us the intense and exceeding truth of his conceptions of nature.   Livy is
instinct with poetry.   Yet Horace, Catullus, Ovid,
10 and generally the other great writers of the Virgilian age, saw man and nature in the mirror of
Greece.   The institutions also, and the religion of
Rome, were less poetical than those of Greece, as
the shadow is less vivid than the substance.   Hence
15 poetry in Rome seemed to follow, rather than
accompany, the perfection of political and domestic
society.   The true poetry of Rome lived in its
institutions ; for whatever of beautiful, of true and
majestic, they contained, could have sprung only
20 from the faculty which creates the order in which
they consist.   The life of Camillus, the death of
Regulus ; the expectation of the senators, in their
godlike state, of the victorious Gauls ; the refusal
of the republic to make peace with Hannibal after
25 the battle of Cannæ, were not the consequences of
a refined calculation of the probable personal
advantage to result from such a rhythm and order
in the shows of life, to those who were at once the
poets and the actors of these immortal dramas.
30 The imagination beholding the beauty of this
order, created it out of itself according to its own
idea ; the consequence was empire, and the reward
everlasting fame.   These things are not the less

poetry *quia carent vate sacro*.   They are the episodes of that cyclic poem written by Time upon
the memories of men.   The Past, like an inspired
rhapsodist, fills the theatre of everlasting generations with their harmony.   5
At length the ancient system of religion and
manners had fulfilled the circle of its evolutions.
And the world would have fallen into utter anarchy
and darkness, but that there were found poets
among the authors of the Christian and chivalric   10
systems of manners and religion, who created
forms of opinion and action never before conceived;
which, copied into the imaginations of men, became as generals to the bewildered armies of their
thoughts.   It is foreign to the present purpose to   15
touch upon the evil produced by these systems;
except that we protest, on the ground of the principles already established, that no portion of it can
be attributed to the poetry they contain.
It is probable that the poetry of Moses, Job,   20
David, Solomon, and Isaiah had produced a great
effect upon the mind of Jesus and his disciples.
The scattered fragments preserved to us by the
biographers of this extraordinary person are all
instinct with the most vivid poetry.   But his doc-   25
trines seem to have been quickly distorted.   At a
certain period after the prevalence of a system of
opinions founded upon those promulgated by him,
the three forms into which Plato had distributed
the faculties of mind underwent a sort of apothe-   30
osis, and became the object of the worship of the
civilized world.   Here it is to be confessed that
" Light " seems to "thicken,"

And the crow makes wing to the rooky wood;
Good things of day begin to droop and drowse,
Whiles night's black agents to their preys do rouse.

But mark how beautiful an order has sprung from
5 the dust and blood of this fierce chaos! how the
world, as from a resurrection, balancing itself .on
the golden wings of knowledge and of hope, has
reassumed its yet unwearied flight into the heaven
of time. Listen to the music, unheard by outward
10 ears, which is as a ceaseless and invisible wind,
nourishing its everlasting course with strength and
swiftness.

The poetry in the doctrines of Jesus Christ, and
the mythology and institutions of the Celtic con-
15 querors of the Roman empire, outlived the darkness and the convulsions connected with their
growth and victory, and blended themselves in a
new fabric of manners and opinion. It is an error
to impute the ignorance of the Dark Ages to the
20 Christian doctrines or the predominance of the
Celtic nations. Whatever of evil their agencies
may have contained sprang from the extinction of
the poetical principle, connected with the progress
of despotism and superstition. Men, from causes
25 too intricate to be here discussed, had become
insensible and selfish ; their own will had become
feeble, and yet they were its slaves, and thence the
slaves of the will of others ; lust, fear, avarice,
cruelty, and fraud, characterized a race amongst
30 whom no one was to be found capable of *creating*
in form, language, or institution. The moral anomalies of such a state of society are not justly to be
charged upon any class of events immediately con-

nected with them, and those events are most
entitled to our approbation which could dissolve it
most expeditiously. It is unfortunate for those
who cannot distinguish words from thoughts, that
many of these anomalies have been incorporated 5
into our popular religion.

It was not until the eleventh century that the
effects of the poetry of the Christian and chivalric
systems began to manifest themselves. The principle of equality had been discovered and applied by 10
Plato in his Republic, as the theoretical rule of the
mode in which the materials of pleasure and of
power produced by the common skill and labor of
human beings ought to be distributed among them.
The limitations of this rule were asserted by him 15
to be determined only by the sensibility of each,
or the utility to result to all. Plato, following the
doctrines of Timæus and Pythagoras, taught also a
moral and intellectual system of doctrine, compre-
hending at once the past, the present, and the 20
future condition of man. Jesus Christ divulged
the sacred and eternal truths contained in these
views to mankind, and Christianity, in its abstract
purity, became the exoteric expression of the
esoteric doctrines of the poetry and wisdom of 25
antiquity. The incorporation of the Celtic nations
with the exhausted population of the south impressed upon it the figure of the poetry existing in
their mythology and institutions. The result was
a sum of the action and reaction of all the causes 30
included in it ; for it may be assumed as a maxim
that no nation or religion can supersede any other
without incorporating into itself a portion of that

which it supersedes. The abolition of personal
and domestic slavery, and the emancipation of
women from a great part of the degrading re-
straints of antiquity, were among the consequences
5 of these events.

The abolition of personal slavery is the basis of
the highest political hope that it can enter into the
mind of man to conceive. The freedom of women
produced the poetry of sexual love. Love became
10 a religion, the idols of whose worship were ever
present. It was as if the statues of Apollo and
the Muses had been endowed with life and motion,
and had walked forth among their worshippers ; so
that earth became peopled by the inhabitants of a
15 diviner world. The familiar appearances and pro-
ceedings of life became wonderful and heavenly,
and a paradise was created as out of the wrecks of
Eden. And as this creation itself is poetry, so its
creators were poets, and language was the instru-
20 ment of their art : "Galeotto fù il libro, e chi lo
scrisse." The Provençal Trouveurs, or inventors,
preceded Petrarch, whose verses are as spells
which unseal the inmost enchanted fountains of
the delight which is in the grief of love. It is
25 impossible to feel them without becoming a portion
of that beauty which we contemplate ; it were
superfluous to explain how the gentleness and
elevation of mind connected with these sacred
emotions can render men more amiable, more gen-
30 erous and wise, and lift them out of the dull vapors
of the little world of self. Dante understood the
secret things of love even more than Petrarch.
His Vita. Nuova is an inexhaustible fountain of

purity of sentiment and language; it is the idealized history of that period and those intervals of
his life which were dedicated to love. His apotheosis of Beatrice in Paradise, and the gradations of
his own love and her loveliness, by which as by 5
steps he feigns himself to have ascended to the
throne of the Supreme Cause, is the most glorious
imagination of modern poetry. The acutest critics
have justly reversed the judgment of the vulgar
and the order of the great acts of the Divina 10
Commedia, in the measure of the admiration which
they accord to the Hell, Purgatory, and Paradise.
The latter is a perpetual hymn of everlasting love.
Love, which found a worthy poet in Plato alone of
all the ancients, has been celebrated by a chorus of 15
the greatest writers of the renovated world; and
the music has penetrated the caverns of society,
and its echoes still drown the dissonance of arms
and superstition. At successive intervals, Ariosto,
Tasso, Shakespeare, Spenser, Calderon, Rousseau, 20
and the great writers of our own age, have celebrated the dominion of love, planting as it were tro-
phies in the human mind of that sublimest victory
over sensuality and force. The true relation borne
to each other by the sexes into which human kind 25
is distributed has become less misunderstood; and
if the error which confounded diversity with inequality of the powers of the two sexes has been
partially recognized in the opinions and institutions
of modern Europe, we owe this great benefit to 30
the worship of which chivalry was the law, and
poets the prophets.

The poetry of Dante may be considered as the

bridge thrown over the stream of time, which
unites the modern and ancient world. The distorted notions of invisible things which Dante and
his rival Milton have idealized, are merely the
5 mask and the mantle in which these great poets
walk through eternity enveloped and disguised. It
is a difficult question to determine how far they
were conscious of the distinction which must have
subsisted in their minds between their own creeds
10 and that of the people.   Dante at least appears to
wish to mark the full extent of it by placing
Riphæus, whom Virgil calls *justissimus unus*, in
Paradise, and observing a most heretical caprice in
his distribution of rewards and punishments.   And
15 Milton's poem contains within itself a philosophical
refutation of that system, of which, by a strange
and natural antithesis, it has been a chief popular
support.   Nothing can exceed the energy and magnificence of the character of Satan as expressed in
20 Paradise Lost.   It is a mistake to suppose that
he could ever have been intended for the popular
personification of evil.   Implacable hate, patient
cunning, and a sleepless refinement of device to
inflict the extremest anguish on an enemy, these
25 things are evil; and, although venial in a slave, are
not to be forgiven in a tyrant; although redeemed
by much that ennobles his defeat in one subdued,
are marked by all that dishonors his conquest in
the victor.   Milton's Devil as a moral being is as
30 far superior to his God, as one who perseveres in
some purpose which he has conceived to be excellent, in spite of adversity and torture, is to one who
in the cold security of undoubted triumph inflicts

the most horrible revenge upon his enemy, not
from any mistaken notion of inducing him to
repent of a perseverance in enmity, but with the
alleged design of exasperating him to deserve new
torments. Milton has so far violated the popular 5
creed (if this shall be judged to be a violation) as
to have alleged no superiority of moral virtue to
his God over his Devil. And this bold neglect of
a direct moral purpose is the most decisive proof
of the supremacy of Milton's genius. He mingled 10
as it were the elements of human nature as colors
upon a single pallet, and arranged them in the
composition of his great picture according to the
laws of epic truth, that is, according to the laws
of that principle by which a series of actions of 15
the external universe and of intelligent and ethical
beings is calculated to excite the sympathy of
succeeding generations of mankind. The Divina
Commedia and Paradise Lost have conferred upon
modern mythology a systematic form ; and when 20
change and time shall have added one more superstition to the mass of those which have arisen and
decayed upon the earth, commentators will be
learnedly employed in elucidating the religion of
ancestral Europe, only not utterly forgotten be- 25
cause it will have been stamped with the eternity
of genius.

Homer was the first and Dante the second epic
poet : that is, the second poet, the series of whose
creations bore a defined and intelligible relation to 30
the knowledge and sentiment and religion of the
age in which he lived, and of the ages which followed it, developing itself in correspondence with

their development. For Lucretius had limed the wings of his swift spirit in the dregs of the sensible world; and Virgil, with a modesty that ill became his genius, had affected the fame of an 5 imitator, even whilst he created anew all that he copied; and none among the flock of mock-birds, though their notes are sweet, Apollonius Rhodius, Quintus (Calaber) Smyrnæus, Nonnus, Lucan, Statius, or Claudian, have sought even to fulfil a single 10 condition of epic truth. Milton was the third epic poet. For if the title of epic in its highest sense be refused to the Æneid, still less can it be conceded to the Orlando Furioso, the Gerusalemme Liberata, the Lusiad, or the Fairy Queen.

15   Dante and Milton were both deeply penetrated with the ancient religion of the civilized world, and its spirit exists in their poetry probably in the same proportion as its forms survived in the unreformed worship of modern Europe. The one pre- 20 ceded and the other followed the Reformation at almost equal intervals. Dante was the first religious reformer, and Luther surpassed him rather in the rudeness and acrimony, than in the boldness of his censures of papal usurpation. Dante was 25 the first awakener of entranced Europe; he created a language, in itself music and persuasion, out of a chaos of inharmonious barbarisms. He was the congregator of those great spirits who presided over the resurrection of learning, the Lucifer 30 of that starry flock which in the thirteenth century shone forth from republican Italy, as from a heaven, into the darkness of the benighted world. His very words are instinct with spirit; each is

as a spark, a burning atom of inextinguishable
thought; and many yet lie covered in the ashes
of their birth, and pregnant with a lightning which
has yet found no conductor. All high poetry is
infinite; it is as the first acorn, which contained all 5
oaks potentially. Veil after veil may be undrawn,
and the inmost naked beauty of the meaning never
exposed. A great poem is a fountain for ever over-
flowing with the waters of wisdom and delight;
and after one person and one age has exhausted all 10
its divine effluence which their peculiar relations
enable them to share, another and yet another succeeds, and new relations are ever developed, the
source of an unforeseen and an unconceived de-
light.   15

The age immediately succeeding to that of
Dante, Petrarch, and Boccaccio, was characterized
by a revival of painting, sculpture, and architecture. Chaucer caught the sacred inspiration, and
the superstructure of English literature is based 20
upon the materials of Italian invention.

But let us not be betrayed from a defense into a
critical history of poetry and its influence on society. Be it enough to have pointed out the effects
of poets, in the large and true sense of the word, 25
upon their own and all succeeding times.

But poets have been challenged to resign the
civic crown to reasoners and mechanists, on another plea. It is admitted that the exercise of the
imagination is most delightful, but it is alleged 30
that that of reason is more useful. Let us exam-
ine, as the grounds of this distinction, what is here
meant by utility. Pleasure or good, in a general

sense, is that which the consciousness of a sensi-
tive and intelligent being seeks, and in which, when
found, it acquiesces. There are two kinds of pleasure, one durable, universal, and permanent ; the
5 other transitory and particular. Utility may either
express the means of producing the former or the
latter. In the former sense, whatever strengthens
and purifies the affections, enlarges the imagination,
and adds spirit to sense, is useful. But a narrower
10 meaning may be assigned to the word utility, con-
fining it to express that which banishes the im-
portunity of the wants of our animal nature, the
surrounding men with security of life, the dispers-
ing the grosser delusions of superstition, and the
15 conciliating such a degree of mutual forbearance
among men as may consist with the motives of
personal advantage.

Undoubtedly the promoters of utility, in this
limited sense, have their appointed office in society.
20 They follow the footsteps of poets, and copy the
sketches of their creations into the book of common life. They make space and give time. Their
exertions are of the highest value, so long as they
confine their administration of the concerns of the
25 inferior powers of our nature within the limits due
to the superior ones. But whilst the sceptic
destroys gross superstitions, let him spare to deface, as some of the French writers have defaced,
the eternal truths charactered upon the imagina-
30 tions of men. Whilst the mechanist abridges, and
the political economist combines labor, let them
beware that their speculations, for want of correspondence with those first principles which belong

to the imagination, do not tend, as they have in modern England, to exasperate at once the extremes of luxury and of want. They have exemplified the saying, "To him that hath, more shall be given; and from him that hath not, the little that 5 he hath shall be taken away." The rich have become richer, and the poor have become poorer; and the vessel of the state is driven between the Scylla and Charybdis of anarchy and despotism. Such are the effects which must ever flow from an 10 unmitigated exercise of the calculating faculty.

It is difficult to define pleasure in its highest sense, the definition involving a number of apparent paradoxes. For, from an inexplicable defect of harmony in the constitution of human nature, the 15 pain of the inferior is frequently connected with the pleasures of the superior portions of our being. Sorrow, terror, anguish, despair itself, are often the chosen expressions of an approximation to the highest good. Our sympathy in tragic fic- 20 tion depends on this principle; tragedy delights by affording a shadow of that pleasure which exists in pain. This is the source also of the melancholy which is inseparable from the sweetest melody. The pleasure that is in sorrow is sweeter than the 25 pleasure of pleasure itself. And hence the saying, "It is better to go to the house of mourning than to the house of mirth." Not that this highest species of pleasure is necessarily linked with pain. The delight of love and friendship, the ecstasy of 30 the admiration of nature, the joy of the perception and still more of the creation of poetry, is often wholly unalloyed.

The production and assurance of pleasure in
this highest sense is true utility. Those who produce and preserve this pleasure are poets or poetical
philosophers.

5   The exertions of Locke, Hume, Gibbon, Voltaire,
Rousseau, and their disciples, in favor of oppressed
and deluded humanity, are entitled to the gratitude
of mankind. Yet it is easy to calculate the degree
of moral and intellectual improvement which the
10 world would have exhibited, had they never lived.
A little more nonsense would have been talked for
a century or two ; and perhaps a few more men,
women, and children burnt as heretics. We might
not at this moment have been congratulating each
15 other on the abolition of the Inquisition in Spain.
But it exceeds all imagination to conceive what
would have been the moral condition of the world
if neither Dante, Petrarch, Boccaccio, Chaucer,
Shakespeare, Calderon, Lord Bacon, nor Milton,
20 had ever existed ; if Raphael and Michael Angelo
had never been born ; if the Hebrew poetry had
never been translated ; if a revival of the study of
Greek literature had never taken place ; if no
monuments of ancient sculpture had been handed
25 down to us ; and if the poetry of the religion of
the ancient world had been extinguished together
with its belief. The human mind could never,
except by the intervention of these excitements,
have been awakened to the invention of the grosser
30 sciences, and that application of analytical reasoning to the aberrations of society which it is now
attempted to exalt over the direct expression of the
inventive and creative faculty itself.

We have more moral, political, and historical wisdom than we know how to reduce into practice; we have more scientific and economical knowledge than can be accommodated to the just distribution of the produce which it multiplies. The poetry 5 in these systems of thought is concealed by the accumulation of facts and calculating processes. There is no want of knowledge respecting what is wisest and best in morals, government, and political economy, or at least what is wiser and better than 10 what men now practise and endure. But we let "*I dare not* wait upon *I would*, like the poor cat in the adage." We want the creative faculty to imagine that which we know; we want the generous impulse to act that which we imagine; we want the 15 poetry of life: our calculations have outrun conception; we have eaten more than we can digest. The cultivation of those sciences which have enlarged the limits of the empire of man over the external world, has, for want of the poetical fac- 20 ulty, proportionally circumscribed those of the internal world; and man, having enslaved the elements, remains himself a slave. To what but a cultivation of the mechanical arts in a degree disproportioned to the presence of the creative faculty, 25 which is the basis of all knowledge, is to be attributed the abuse of all invention for abridging and combining labor, to the exasperation of the inequality of mankind? From what other cause has it arisen that the discoveries which should have 30 lightened, have added a weight to the curse imposed on Adam? Poetry, and the principle of Self of which money is the visible incarnation, are the God and Mammon of the world.

The functions of the poetical faculty are two-fold : by one it creates new materials of knowledge,
5 and power, and pleasure ; by the other it engenders in the mind a desire to reproduce and arrange them according to a certain rhythm and order which may be called the beautiful and the good. The cultivation of poetry is never more to be desired than at
10 periods when, from an excess of the selfish and calculating principle, the accumulation of the materials of external life exceed the quantity of the power of assimilating them to the internal laws of human nature. The body has then become too
15 unwieldy for that which animates it.

Poetry is indeed something divine. It is at once the centre and circumference of knowledge; it is that which comprehends all science, and that to which all science must be referred. It is at the
20 same time the root and blossom of all other systems of thought ; it is that from which all spring, and that which adorns all ; and that which, if blighted, denies the fruit and the seed, and withholds from the barren world the nourishment and
25 the succession of the scions of the tree of life. It is the perfect and consummate surface and bloom of all things ; it is as the odor and the color of the rose to the texture of the elements which compose it, as the form and splendor of unfaded
30 beauty to the secrets of anatomy and corruption. What were virtue, love, patriotism, friendship ; what were the scenery of this beautiful universe which we inhabit ; what were our consolations on

this side of the grave, and what were our aspirations beyond it, — if poetry did not ascend to bring light and fire from those eternal regions where the owl-winged faculty of calculation dare not ever soar? Poetry is not like reasoning, a power to be 5 exerted according to the determination of the will. A man cannot say, "I will compose poetry." The greatest poet even cannot say it; for the mind in creation is as a fading coal, which some invisible influence, like an inconstant wind, awakens to tran- 10 sitory brightness; this power arises from within, like the color of a flower which fades and changes as it is developed, and the conscious portions of our natures are unprophetic either of its approach or its departure. Could this influence be durable 15 in its original purity and force, it is impossible to predict the greatness of the results; but when composition begins, inspiration is already on the decline, and the most glorious poetry that has ever been communicated to the world is probably a 20 feeble shadow of the original conceptions of the poet. I appeal to the greatest poets of the present day whether it is not an error to assert that the finest passages of poetry are produced by labor and study. The toil and the delay recommended by 25 critics can be justly interpreted to mean no more than a careful observation of the inspired moments, and an artificial connection of the spaces between their suggestions by the intertexture of conventional expressions — a necessity only imposed by 30 the limitedness of the poetical faculty itself; for Milton conceived the Paradise Lost as a whole before he executed it in portions. We have his

own authority also for the muse having "dictated"
to him the "unpremeditated song."   And let this
be an answer to those who would allege the fifty-six
various readings of the first line of the Orlando
5 Furioso.   Compositions so produced are to poetry
what mosaic is to painting.   The instinct and in-
tuition of the poetical faculty is still more observable in the plastic and pictorial arts : a great statue
or picture grows under the power of the artist as a
10 child in the mother's womb ; and the very mind
which directs the hands in formation, is incapable
of accounting to itself for the origin, the gradations, or the media of the process.

Poetry is the record of the best and happiest
15 moments of the happiest and best minds.   We are
aware of evanescent visitations of thought and
feeling, sometimes associated with place or person,
sometimes regarding our own mind alone, and
always arising unforeseen and departing unbidden,
20 but elevating and delightful beyond all expression ;
so that even in the desire and the regret they leave,
there cannot but be pleasure, participating as it
does in the nature of its object.   It is as it were
the interpenetration of a diviner nature through our
25 own ; but its footsteps are like those of a wind
over the sea, which the morning calm erases, and
whose traces remain only, as on the wrinkled sand
which paves it.   These and corresponding conditions
of being are experienced principally by those of
30 the most delicate sensibility and the most enlarged
imagination ; and the state of mind produced by
them is at war with every base desire.   The enthusiasm of virtue, love, patriotism, and friendship

is essentially linked with such emotions; and
whilst they last, self appears as what it is, an atom
to a universe. Poets are not only subject to these
experiences as spirits of the most refined organiza-
tion, but they can color all that they combine with 5
the evanescent hues of this ethereal world; a
word, a trait in the representation of a scene or a
passion will touch the enchanted chord, and rean-
imate, in those who have ever experienced these
emotions, the sleeping, the cold, the buried image 10
of the past. Poetry thus makes immortal all that
is best and most beautiful in the world; it arrests
the vanishing apparitions which haunt the inter-
lunations of life, and veiling them or in language
or in form, sends them forth among mankind, bear- 15
ing sweet news of kindred joy to those with whom
their sisters abide — abide, because there is no por-
tal of expression from the caverns of the spirit
which they inhabit into the universe of things.
Poetry redeems from decay the visitations of the 20
divinity in man.

Poetry turns all things to loveliness ; it exalts the
beauty of that which is most beautiful, and it adds
beauty to that which is most deformed ; it marries
exultation and horror, grief and pleasure, eternity 25
and change ; it subdues to union under its light
yoke all irreconcilable things. It transmutes all
that it touches, and every form moving within the
radiance of its presence is changed by wondrous
sympathy to an incarnation of the spirit which it 30
breathes ; its secret alchemy turns to potable gold
the poisonous waters which flow from death
through life ; it strips the veil of familiarity from

the world, and lays bare the naked and sleeping beauty which is the spirit of its forms.

All things exist as they are perceived : at least in relation to the percipient.

5   The mind is its own place, and in itself
       Can make a Heaven of Hell, a Hell of Heaven.

But poetry defeats the curse which binds us to be subjected to the accident of surrounding impressions. And whether it spreads its own figured
10 curtain, or withdraws life's dark veil from before the scene of things, it equally creates for us a being within our being. It makes us the inhabitant of a world to which the familiar world is a chaos. It reproduces the common universe of
15 which we are portions and percipients, and it purges from our inward sight the film of familiarity which obscures from us the wonder of our being. It compels us to feel that which we perceive, and to imagine that which we know. It
20 creates anew the universe, after it has been annihilated in our minds by the recurrence of impressions blunted by reiteration. It justifies the bold and true word of Tasso: *Non merita nome di*
| *creatore, se non Iddio ed il Poeta.*
25   A poet, as he is the author to others of the highest wisdom, pleasure, virtue, and glory, so he ought personally to be the happiest, the best, the wisest, and the most illustrious of men. As to his glory, let time be challenged to declare whether the fame
30 of any other institutor of human life be comparable to that of a poet. That he is the wisest, the happiest, and the best, inasmuch as he is a poet, is equally incontrovertible : the greatest poets

have been men of the most spotless virtue, of the
most consummate prudence, and, if we would look
into the interior of their lives, the most fortunate
of men ; and the exceptions, as they regard those
who possessed the poetic faculty in a high yet 5
inferior degree, will be found on consideration to
confirm rather than destroy the rule. Let us for a
moment stoop to the arbitration of popular breath,
and usurping and uniting in our own persons the
incompatible characters of accuser, witness, judge, 10
and executioner, let us decide without trial, testimony, or form, that certain motives of those who
are "there sitting where we dare not soar," are
reprehensible. Let us assume that Homer was a
drunkard, that Virgil was a flatterer, that Horace 15
was a coward, that Tasso was a madman, that Lord
Bacon was a peculator, that Raphael was a liber-
tine, that Spenser was a poet laureate. It is inconsistent with this division of our subject to cite
living poets, but posterity has done ample justice 20
to the great names now referred to. Their errors
have been weighed and found to have been dust
in the balance ; if their sins were as scarlet,
they are now white as snow ; they have been
washed in the blood of the mediator and redeemer, 25
Time. Observe in what a ludicrous chaos the imputations of real or fictitious crime have been con-
fused in the contemporary calumnies against poetry
and poets ; consider how little is as it appears —
or appears as it is ; look to your own motives, and 30
judge not, lest ye be judged.

Poetry, as has been said, differs in this respect
from logic, that it is not subject to the control of the

active powers of the mind, and that its birth and
recurrence have no necessary connection with the
consciousness or will. It is presumptuous to determine that these are the necessary conditions of all
5 mental causation, when mental effects are experienced insusceptible of being referred to them.
The frequent recurrence of the poetical power, it
is obvious to suppose, may produce in the mind a
habit of order and harmony correlative with its
10 own nature and with its effects upon other minds.
But in the intervals of inspiration — and they may
be frequent without being durable — a poet becomes
a man, and is abandoned to the sudden reflux of
the influences under which others habitually live.
15 But as he is more delicately organized than other
men, and sensible to pain and pleasure, both his
own and that of others, in a degree unknown to
them, he will avoid the one and pursue the other
with an ardor proportioned to this difference. And
20 he renders himself obnoxious to calumny when he
neglects to observe the circumstances under which
these objects of universal pursuit and flight have
disguised themselves in one another's garments.

But there is nothing necessarily evil in this
25 error, and thus cruelty, envy, revenge, avarice, and
the passions purely evil, have never formed any portion of the popular imputations on the lives of poets.

I have thought it most favorable to the cause of
truth to set down these remarks according to the
30 order in which they were suggested to my mind,
by a consideration of the subject itself, instead of
observing the formality of a polemical reply ; but if
the view which they contain be just, they will be

found to involve a refutation of the arguers against
poetry, so far at least as regards the first division
of the subject. I can readily conjecture what
should have moved the gall of some learned and
intelligent writers who quarrel with certain versi- 5
fiers ; I, like them, confess myself unwilling to be
stunned by the Theseids of the hoarse Codri of
the day. Bavius and Mævius undoubtedly are, as
they ever were, insufferable persons. But it be-
longs to a philosophical critic to distinguish rather 10
than confound.

The first part of these remarks has related to
poetry in its elements and principles ; and it has
been shown, as well as the narrow limits assigned
them would permit, that what is called poetry in 15
a restricted sense, has a common source with all
other forms of order and of beauty according to
which the materials of human life are susceptible
of being arranged, and which is poetry in a universal sense.   20

The second part will have for its object an application of these principles to the present state of
the cultivation of poetry, and a defense of the
attempt to idealize the modern forms of manners
and opinions, and compel them into a subordination 25
to the imaginative and creative faculty. For the
literature of England, an energetic development of
which has ever preceded or accompanied a great
and free development of the national will, has
arisen as it were from a new birth. In spite of the 30
low-thoughted envy which would undervalue contemporary merit, our own will be a memorable age
in intellectual achievements, and we live among

such philosophers and poets as surpass beyond comparison any who have appeared since the last national struggle for civil and religious liberty. The most unfailing herald, companion, and follower of the awakening of a great people to work a beneficial change in opinion or institution, is poetry. At such periods there is an accumulation of the power of communicating and receiving intense and impassioned conceptions respecting man and nature.   The persons in whom this power resides may often, as far as regards many portions of their nature, have little apparent correspondence with that spirit of good of which they are the ministers. But even whilst they deny and abjure, they are yet compelled to serve the power which is seated on the throne of their own soul.   It is impossible to read the compositions of the most celebrated writers of the present day without being startled with the electric life which burns within their words.   They measure the circumference and sound the depths of human nature with a comprehensive and all-penetrating spirit, and they are themselves perhaps the most sincerely astonished at its manifestations; for it is less their spirit than the spirit of the age.   Poets are the hierophants of an unapprehended inspiration; the mirrors of the gigantic shadows which futurity casts upon the present; the words which express what they understand not ; the trumpets which sing to battle and feel not what they inspire; the influence which is moved not, but moves.   Poets are the unacknowledged legislators of the world.

THE FOUR AGES OF POETRY.

BY THOMAS LOVE PEACOCK.

Qui inter hæc nutriuntur non magis sapere possunt, quam bene olere qui in culina habitant. — PETRONIUS.

POETRY, like the world, may be said to have four ages, but in a different order: the first age of poetry being the age of iron; the second of gold; the third of silver; and the fourth of brass.

The first, or iron age of poetry, is that in which rude bards 5 celebrate in rough numbers the exploits of ruder chiefs, in days when every man is a warrior, and when the great practical maxim of every form of society, "to keep what we have and to catch what we can," is not yet disguised under names of justice and forms of law, but is the naked motto of the 10 naked sword, which is the only judge and jury in every question of *meum* and *tuum* [mine and thine]. In these days, the only three trades flourishing (besides that of priest, which flourishes always) are those of king, thief, and beggar; the beggar being, for the most part, a king deject, and the thief 15 a king expectant. The first question asked of a stranger is, whether he is a beggar or a thief;[1] the stranger, in reply, usually assumes the first, and awaits a convenient opportunity to prove his claim to the second appellation.

The natural desire of every man to engross to himself as 20 much power and property as he can acquire by any of the means which might makes right, is accompanied by the no less natural desire of making known to as many people as possible the extent to which he has been a winner in this universal game. The successful warrior becomes a chief; the 25

---

[1] See the Odyssey, passim, and Thucydides, I. 5. [Peacock's Note.]

successful chief becomes a king; his next want is an organ
to disseminate the fame of his achievements and the extent
of his possessions, and this organ he finds in a bard, who is
always ready to celebrate the strength of his arm, being first
5 duly inspired by that of his liquor. This is the origin of
poetry, which, like all other trades, takes its rise in the demand for the commodity, and flourishes in proportion to the
extent of the market.

Poetry is thus in its origin panegyrical. The first rude
10 songs of all nations appear to be a sort of brief historical
notices, in a strain of tumid hyperbole, of the exploits and
possessions of a few pre-eminent individuals. They tell us
how many battles such an one has fought, how many helmets
he has cleft, how many breastplates he has pierced, how many
15 widows he has made, how much land he has appropriated,
how many houses he has demolished for other people, what
a large one he has built for himself, how much gold he has
stowed away in it, and how liberally and plentifully he pays,
feeds, and intoxicates the divine and immortal bards, the
20 sons of Jupiter, but for whose everlasting songs the names of
heroes would perish.

This is the first stage of poetry before the invention of
written letters. The numerical modulation is at once useful
as a help to memory, and pleasant to the ears of uncultured
25 men, who are easily caught by sound; and, from the exceeding
flexibility of the yet unformed language, the poet does no
violence to his ideas in subjecting them to the fetters of
number. The savage, indeed, lisps in numbers, and all rude
and uncivilized people express themselves in the manner
30 which we call poetical.

The scenery by which he is surrounded, and the superstitions which are the creed of his age, form the poet's mind.
Rocks, mountains, seas, unsubdued forests, unnavigable
rivers, surround him with forms of power and mystery, which
35 ignorance and fear have peopled with spirits, under multifari-
ous names of gods, goddesses, nymphs, genii, and dæmons.
Of all these personages marvelous tales are in existence: the
nymphs are not indifferent to handsome young men, and the
gentlemen-genii are much troubled and very troublesome

with a propensity to be rude to pretty maidens; the bard, therefore, finds no difficulty in tracing the genealogy of his chief to any of the deities in his neighborhood with whom the said chief may be desirous of claiming relationship.

In this pursuit, as in all others, some, of course, will attain ₅ a very marked pre-eminence; and these will be held in high honor, like Demodocus in the Odyssey, and will be consequently inflated with boundless vanity, like Thamyris in the Iliad. Poets are as yet the only historians and chroniclers of their time, and the sole depositories of all the knowledge ₁₀ of their age; and though this knowledge is rather a crude congeries of traditional fantasies than a collection of useful truths, yet, such as it is, they have it to themselves. They are observing and thinking, while others are robbing and fighting; and though their object be nothing more than to ₁₅ secure a share of the spoil, yet they accomplish this end by intellectual, not by physical power; their success excites emulation to the attainment of intellectual eminence; thus they sharpen their own wits and awaken those of others, at the same time that they gratify vanity and amuse curiosity. ₂₀ A skilful display of the little knowledge they have gains them credit for the possession of much more which they have not. Their familiarity with the secret history of gods and genii obtains for them, without much difficulty, the reputation of inspiration; thus they are not only historians, but theolo- ₂₅ gians, moralists, and legislators; delivering their oracles *ex cathedra* [from the chair of authority], and being indeed often themselves (as Orpheus and Amphion) regarded as portions and emanations of divinity; building cities with a song, and leading brutes with a symphony — which are only metaphors ₃₀ for the faculty of leading multitudes by the nose.

The golden age of poetry finds its materials in the age of iron. This age begins when poetry begins to be retrospective; when something like a more extended system of civil polity is established; when personal strength and courage ₃₅ avail less to the aggrandizing of their possessor, and to the making and marring of kings and kingdoms, and are checked by organized bodies, social institutions, and hereditary successions. Men also live more in the light of truth and within

the interchange of observation, and thus perceive that the
agency of gods and genii is not so frequent among themselves as, to judge from the songs and legends of the past
time, it was among their ancestors. From these two circum-
5 stances — really diminished personal power, and apparently
diminished familiarity with gods and genii — they very easily
and naturally deduce two conclusions: 1st, That men are
degenerated, and 2nd, That they are less in favor with the
gods. The people of the petty states and colonies, which
10 have now acquired stability and form, which owed their origin
and first prosperity to the talents and courage of a single
chief, magnify their founder through the mists of distance
and tradition, and perceive him achieving wonders with a
god or goddess always at his elbow. They find his name
15 and his exploits thus magnified and accompanied in their
traditionary songs, which are their only memorials. All that
is said of him is in this character. There is nothing to con-
tradict it. The man and his exploits and his tutelary deities
are mixed and blended in one invariable association. The
20 marvelous, too, is very much like a snowball: it grows as it
rolls downward, till the little nucleus of truth, which began
its descent from the summit, is hidden in the accumulation
of superinduced hyperbole.

When tradition, thus adorned and exaggerated, has sur-
25 rounded the founders of families and states with so much
adventitious power and magnificence, there is no praise
which a living poet can, without fear of being kicked for
clumsy flattery, address to a living chief, that will not still
leave the impression that the latter is not so great a man as
30 his ancestors. The man must, in this case, be praised
through his ancestors. Their greatness must be established,
and he must be shown to be their worthy descendant. All
the people of a state are interested in the founder of their
state. All states that have harmonized into a common form
35 of society are interested in their respective founders. All
men are interested in their ancestors. All men love to look
back into the days that are past. In these circumstances
traditional national poetry is reconstructed, and brought, like
chaos, into order and form. The interest is more universal;

understanding is enlarged : passion still has scope and play;
character is still various and strong; nature is still unsubdued and existing in all her beauty and magnificence, and
men are not yet excluded from her observation by the mag-
nitude of cities, or the daily confinement of civic life; poetry 5
is more an art; it requires greater skill in numbers, greater
command of language, more extensive and various knowledge,
and greater comprehensiveness of mind. It still exists without rivals in any other department of literature; and even
the arts, painting and sculpture certainly, and music probably, 10
are comparatively rude and imperfect. The whole field of
intellect is its own. It has no rivals in history, nor in philosophy, nor in science. It is cultivated by the greatest intel-
lects of the age, and listened to by all the rest. This is the
age of Homer, the golden age of poetry. Poetry has now 15
attained its perfection; it has attained the point which it cannot pass; genius therefore seeks new forms for the treatment
of the same subjects; hence the lyric poetry of Pindar and
Alcæus, and the tragic poetry of Æschylus and Sophocles.
The favor of kings, the honor of the Olympic crown, the 20
applause of present multitudes, all that can feed vanity and
stimulate rivalry, await the successful cultivator of this art,
till its forms become exhausted, and new rivals arise around
it in new fields of literature, which gradually acquire more
influence as, with the progress of reason and civilization, 25
facts become more interesting than fiction; indeed, the
maturity of poetry may be considered the infancy of history.
The transition from Homer to Herodotus is scarcely more
remarkable than that from Herodotus to Thucydides, in the
gradual dereliction of fabulous incident and ornamented lan- 30
guage. Herodotus is as much a poet in relation to Thucydides as Homer is in relation to Herodotus. The history of
Herodotus is half a poem; it was written while the whole
field of literature yet belonged to the Muses, and the nine
books of which it was composed were therefore of right, as 35
well as of courtesy, superinscribed with their nine names.

Speculations, too, and disputes, on the nature of man and
of mind, on moral duties and on good and evil, on the ani-
mate and inanimate components of the visible world, begin to

share attention with the eggs of Leda and the horns of Io, and to draw off from poetry a portion of its once undivided audience.

Then comes the silver age, or the poetry of civilized life. 5 This poetry is of two kinds, imitative and original. The imitative consists in recasting, and giving an exquisite polish to, the poetry of the age of gold; of this Virgil is the most obvious and striking example. The original is chiefly comic, didactic, or satiric, as in Menander, Aristophanes, Horace, 10 and Juvenal. The poetry of this age is characterized by an exquisite and fastidious selection of words, and a labor-d and somewhat monotonous harmony of expression; but its monotony consists in this, that experience having exhausted all the varieties of modulation, the civilized poetry selects the 15 most beautiful, and prefers the repetition of these to ranging through the variety of all. But the best expression being that into which the idea naturally falls, it requires the utmost labor and care so to reconcile the inflexibility of civilized language and the labored polish of versification with the idea 20 intended to be expressed, that sense may not appear to be sacrificed to sound. Hence numerous efforts and rare success.

This state of poetry is, however, a step towards its extinction. Feeling and passion are best painted in, and roused by, ornamental and figurative language; but the reason and 25 the understanding are best addressed in the simplest and most unvarnished phrase. Pure reason and dispassionate truth would be perfectly ridiculous in verse, as we may judge by versifying one of Euclid's demonstrations. This will be found true of all dispassionate reasoning whatever, and of 30 all reasoning that requires comprehensive views and enlarged combinations. It is only the more tangible points of morality, those which command assent at once, those which have a mirror in every mind, and in which the severity of reason is warmed and rendered palatable by being mixed up with 35 feeling and imagination, that are applicable even to what is called moral poetry; and as the sciences of morals and of mind advance towards perfection, as they become more enlarged and comprehensive in their views, as reason gains the ascendancy in them over imagination and feeling, poetry

can no longer accompany them in their progress, but drops
into the background, and leaves them to advance alone.
Thus the empire of thought is withdrawn from poetry, as
the empire of facts had been before. In respect of the latter,
the poet of the age of iron celebrates the achievements of 5
his contemporaries; the poet of the age of gold celebrates
the heroes of the age of iron; the poet of the age of silver
recasts the poems of the age of gold; we may here see how
very slight a ray of historical truth is sufficient to dissipate
all the illusions of poetry. We know no more of the men 10
than of the gods of the Iliad, no more of Achilles than we do
of Thetis, no more of Hector and Andromache than we do of
Vulcan and Venus; these belong altogether to poetry; history
has no share in them; but Virgil knew better than to write
an epic about Cæsar; he left him to Livy, and traveled out 15
of the confines of truth and history into the regions of poetry
and fiction.

Good sense and elegant learning, conveyed in polished and
somewhat monotonous verse, are the perfection of the original
and imitative poetry of civilized life. Its range is limited, 20
and when exhausted, nothing remains but the *crambe repetita*
[stale repetition] of commonplace, which at length becomes
thoroughly wearisome, even to the most indefatigable readers
of the newest new nothings.

It is now evident that poetry must either cease to be culti- 25
vated, or strike into a new path. The poets of the age of
gold have been imitated and repeated till no new imitation
will attract notice; the limited range of ethical and didactic
poetry is exhausted; the associations of daily life in an ad-
vanced state of society are of very dry, methodical, unpoetical 30
matters-of-fact; but there is always a multitude of listless
idlers, yawning for amusement, and gaping for novelty; and
the poet makes it his glory to be foremost among their
purveyors.

Then comes the age of brass, which, by rejecting the polish 35
and the learning of the age of silver, and taking a retrograde
stride to the barbarisms and crude traditions of the age of
iron, professes to return to nature and revive the age of gold.
This is the second childhood of poetry. To the comprehen-

sive energy of the Homeric Muse, which, by giving at once
the grand outline of things, presented to the mind a vivid
picture in one or two verses, inimitable alike in simplicity and
magnificence, is substituted a verbose and minutely-detailed
5 description of thoughts, passions, actions, persons, and
things, in that loose, rambling style of verse, which any one
may write *stans pede in uno* [standing on one foot], at the
rate of two hundred lines in an hour. To this age may be
referred all the poets who flourished in the decline of the
10 Roman Empire. The best specimen of it, though not the
most generally known, is the Dionysiaca of Nonnus, which
contains many passages of exceeding beauty in the midst of
masses of amplification and repetition.

The iron age of classical poetry may be called the bardic;
15 the golden, the Homeric; the silver, the Virgilian; and the
brass, the Nonnic.

Modern poetry has also its four ages; but "it wears its
rue with a difference."

To the age of brass in the ancient world succeeded the
20 Dark Ages, in which the light of the Gospel began to spread
over Europe, and in which, by a mysterious and inscrutable
dispensation, the darkness thickened with the progress of the
light. The tribes that overran the Roman Empire brought
back the days of barbarism, but with this difference, that
25 there were many books in the world, many places in which
they were preserved, and occasionally some one by whom
they were read, who indeed (if he escaped being burned, *pour
l'amour de Dieu* [for the love of God]) generally lived an
object of mysterious fear, with the reputation of magician,
30 alchemist, and astrologer. The emerging of the nations of
Europe from this superinduced barbarism, and their settling
into new forms of polity, was accompanied, as the first ages
of Greece had been, with a wild spirit of adventure, which,
co-operating with new manners and new superstitions, raised
35 up a fresh crop of chimeras, not less fruitful, though far less
beautiful, than those of Greece. The semi-deification of
women by the maxims of the age of chivalry, combining with
these new fables, produced the romance of the Middle Ages.
The founders of the new line of heroes took the place of the

demigods of Grecian poetry. Charlemagne and his Paladins, Arthur and his Knights of the Round Table, the heroes of the iron age of chivalrous poetry, were seen through the same magnifying mist of distance, and their exploits were celebrated with even more extravagant hyperbole. These legends, com- 5 bined with the exaggerated love that pervades the songs of the troubadours, the reputation of magic that attached to learned men, the infant wonders of natural philosophy, the crazy fanaticism of the Crusades, the power and privileges of the great feudal chiefs, and the holy mysteries of monks and 10 nuns, formed a state of society in which no two laymen could meet without fighting, and in which the three staple ingredients of lover, prize-fighter, and fanatic, that composed the basis of the character of every true man, were mixed up and diversified, in different individuals and classes, with so many 15 distinctive excellences, and under such an infinite motley variety of costume, as gave the range of a most extensive and picturesque field to the two great constituents of poetry, love and battle.

From these ingredients of the iron age of modern poetry, 20 dispersed in the rimes of minstrels and the songs of the troubadours, arose the golden age, in which the scattered materials were harmonized and blended about the time of the revival of learning; but with this peculiar difference, that Greek and Roman literature pervaded all the poetry of the golden age of 25 modern poetry, and hence resulted a heterogeneous compound of all ages and nations in one picture; an infinite license, which gave to the poet the free range of the whole field of imagination and memory. This was carried very far by Ariosto, but farthest of all by Shakespeare and his contemporaries, 30 who used time and locality merely because they could not do without them, because every action must have its when and where; but they made no scruple of deposing a Roman Emperor by an Italian Count, and sending him off in the disguise of a French pilgrim to be shot with a blunderbuss by an 35 English archer. This makes the old English drama very picturesque, at any rate, in the variety of costume, and very diversified in action and character, though it is a picture of nothing that ever was seen on earth except a Venetian carnival.

The greatest of English poets, Milton, may be said to stand
alone between the ages of gold and silver, combining the excellences of both; for with all the energy, and power, and
freshness of the first, he united all the studied and elaborate
5 magnificence of the second.

The silver age succeeded, — beginning with Dryden, coming
to perfection with Pope, and ending with Goldsmith, Collins,
and Gray.

Cowper divested verse of its exquisite polish; he thought in
10 metre, but paid more attention to his thoughts than his verse.
It would be difficult to draw the boundary of prose and blank
verse between his letters and his poetry.

The silver age was the reign of authority; but authority
now began to be shaken, not only in poetry but in the whole
15 sphere of its dominion. The contemporaries of Gray and
Cowper were deep and elaborate thinkers. The subtle scep-
ticism of Hume, the solemn irony of Gibbon, the daring paradoxes of Rousseau, and the biting ridicule of Voltaire, directed
the energies of four extraordinary minds to shake every por-
20 tion of the reign of authority. Inquiry was roused, the activity
of intellect was excited, and poetry came in for its share of
the general result. The changes had been rung on lovely
maid and sylvan shade, summer heat and green retreat, wav-
ing trees and sighing breeze, gentle swains and amorous
25 pains, by versifiers who took them on trust as meaning something very soft and tender, without much caring what; but
with this general activity of intellect came a necessity for even
poets to appear to know something of what they professed
to talk of. Thomson and Cowper looked at the trees and hills
30 which so many ingenious gentlemen had rimed about so long
without looking at them at all, and the effect of the operation
on poetry was like the discovery of a new world. Painting
shared the influence, and the principles of picturesque beauty
were explored by adventurous essayists with indefatigable per-
35 tinacity. The success which attended these experiments, and
the pleasure which resulted from them, had the usual effect of
all new enthusiasms, that of turning the heads of a few unfortunate persons, the patriarchs of the age of brass, who, mis-
taking the prominent novelty for the all-important totality,

seem to have ratiocinated much in the following manner:
"Poetical genius is the finest of all things, and we feel that
we have more of it than any one ever had. The way to bring
it to perfection is to cultivate poetical impressions exclusively.
Poetical impressions can be received only among natural 5
scenes, for all that is artificial is anti-poetical. Society is artificial, therefore we will live out of society. The mountains are
natural, therefore we will live in the mountains. There we
shall be shining models of purity and virtue, passing the whole
day in the innocent and amiable occupation of going up and 10
down hill, receiving poetical impressions, and communicating them in immortal verse to admiring generations." To
some such perversion of intellect we owe that egregious
confraternity of rimesters, known by the name of the Lake
Poets; who certainly did receive and communicate to the 15
world some of the most extraordinary poetical impressions
that ever were heard of, and ripened into models of public
virtue, too splendid to need illustration. They wrote verses
on a new principle; saw rocks and rivers in a new light; and
remaining studiously ignorant of history, society, and human 20
nature, cultivated the fantasy only at the expense of the
memory and the reason; and contrived, though they had
retreated from the world for the express purpose of seeing
nature as she was, to see her only as she was not, converting
the land they lived in into a sort of fairyland, which they 25
peopled with mysticisms and chimeras. This gave what is
called a new tone to poetry, and conjured up a herd of desper-
ate imitators, who have brought the age of brass prematurely
to its dotage.

The descriptive poetry of the present day has been called 30
by its cultivators a return to nature. Nothing is more im-
pertinent than this pretension. Poetry cannot travel out of
the regions of its birth, the uncultivated lands of semi-civilized
men. Mr. Wordsworth, the great leader of the returners to
nature, cannot describe a scene under his own eyes without 35
putting into it the shadow of a Danish boy or the living
ghost of Lucy Gray, or some similar fantastical parturition of
the moods of his own mind.

In the origin and perfection of poetry, all the associations

of life were composed of poetical materials. With us it is
decidedly the reverse. We know, too, that there are no
Dryads in Hyde Park, nor Naiads in the Regent's Canal. But
barbaric manners and supernatural interventions are essential
5 to poetry. Either in the scene, or in the time, or in both, it
must be remote from our ordinary perceptions. While the
historian and the philosopher are advancing in, and acceler-
ating, the progress of knowledge, the poet is wallowing in the
rubbish of departed ignorance, and raking up the ashes of
10 dead savages to find gewgaws and rattles for the grown
babies of the age. Mr. Scott digs up the poachers and cattle-
stealers of the ancient border. Lord Byron cruises for thieves
and pirates on the shores of the Morea and among the Greek
islands. Mr. Southey wades through ponderous volumes of
15 travels and old chronicles, from which he carefully selects all
that is false, useless, and absurd, as being essentially poetical ;
and when he has a commonplace book full of monstrosities,
strings them into an epic. Mr. Wordsworth picks up village
legends from old women and sextons ; and Mr. Coleridge, to
20 the valuable information acquired from similar sources, super-
adds the dreams of crazy theologians and the mysticisms of
German metaphysics, and favors the world with visions in
verse, in which the quadruple elements of sexton, old woman,
Jeremy Taylor, and Immanuel Kant are harmonized into a
25 delicious poetical compound. Mr. Moore presents us with
a Persian, and Mr. Campbell with a Pennsylvanian tale, both
formed on the same principle as Mr. Southey's epics, by
extracting from a perfunctory and desultory perusal of a
collection of voyages and travels, all that useful investigation
30 would not seek for and that common sense would reject.
　　These disjointed relics of tradition and fragments of second-
hand observation, being woven into a tissue of verse, con-
structed on what Mr. Coleridge calls a new principle (that is,
no principle at all), compose a modern-antique compound of
35 frippery and barbarism, in which the puling sentimentality
of the present time is grafted on the misrepresented rugged-
ness of the past into a heterogeneous congeries of unamalga-
mating manners, sufficient to impose on the common readers
of poetry, over whose understandings the poet of this class

possesses that commanding advantage which, in all circumstances and conditions of life, a man who knows something,
however little, always possesses over one who knows nothing.
   A poet in our times is a semi-barbarian in a civilized community. He lives in the days that are past. His ideas, 5
thoughts, feelings, associations, are all with barbarous manners, obsolete customs, and exploded superstitions. The
march of his intellect is like that of a crab, backward. The
brighter the light diffused around him by the progress of
reason, the thicker is the darkness of antiquated barbarism 10
in which he buries himself like a mole, to throw up the barren
hillocks of his Cimmerian labors. The philosophic mental
tranquillity which looks round with an equal eye on all external
things, collects a store of ideas, discriminates their relative
value, assigns to all their proper place, and from the materials 15
of useful knowledge thus collected, appreciated, and arranged,
forms new combinations that impress the stamp of their
power and utility on the real business of life, is diametrically
the reverse of that frame of mind which poetry inspires, or
from which poetry can emanate. The highest inspirations 20
of poetry are resolvable into three ingredients: the rant of
unregulated passion, the whining of exaggerated feeling, and
the cant of factitious sentiment; and can therefore serve only
to ripen a splendid lunatic like Alexander, a puling driveler
like Werter, or a morbid dreamer like Wordsworth. It can 25
never make a philosopher, nor a statesman, nor in any class
of life a useful or rational man. It cannot claim the slightest
share in any one of the comforts and utilities of life, of
which we have witnessed so many and so rapid advances.
But though not useful, it may be said it is highly ornamental, 30
and deserves to be cultivated for the pleasure it yields.
Even if this be granted, it does not follow that a writer of
poetry in the present state of society is not a waster of his
own time, and a robber of that of others. Poetry is not one
of those arts which, like painting, require repetition and 35
multiplication, in order to be diffused among society. There
are more good poems already existing than are sufficient to
employ that portion of life which any mere reader and recipi-
ent of poetical impressions should devote to them, and these,

having been produced in poetical times, are far superior in all the characteristics of poetry to the artificial reconstructions of a few morbid ascetics in unpoetical times. To read the promiscuous rubbish of the present time, to the exclusion of the
5 select treasures of the past, is to substitute the worse for the better variety of the same mode of enjoyment.

But in whatever degree poetry is cultivated, it must necessarily be to the neglect of some branch of useful study; and it is a lamentable spectacle to see minds capable of better things
10 running to seed in the specious indolence of these empty, aimless mockeries of intellectual exertion. Poetry was the mental rattle that awakened the attention of intellect in the infancy of civil society; but for the maturity of mind to make a serious business of the playthings of its childhood, is as
15 absurd as for a full-grown man to rub his gums with coral, and cry to be charmed to sleep by the jingle of silver bells.

As to that small portion of our contemporary poetry which is neither descriptive, nor narrative, nor dramatic, and which, for want of a better name, may be called ethical, the most
20 distinguished portion of it, consisting merely of querulous, egotistical rhapsodies, to express the writer's high dissatisfaction with the world and everything in it, serves only to confirm what has been said of the semi-barbarous character of poets, who from singing dithyrambics and "Io Triumphe,"
25 while society was savage, grow rabid, and out of their element, as it becomes polished and enlightened.

Now when we consider that it is not to the thinking and studious, and scientific and philosophical part of the community, not to those whose minds are bent on the pursuit
30 and promotion of permanently useful ends and aims, that poets must address their minstrelsy, but to that much larger portion of the reading public whose minds are not awakened to the desire of valuable knowledge, and who are indifferent to anything beyond being charmed, moved, excited, affected,
35 and exalted, — charmed by harmony, moved by sentiment, excited by passion, affected by pathos, and exalted by sublimity, — harmony, which is language on the rack of Procrustes; sentiment, which is canting egotism in the mask of refined feeling; passion, which is the commotion of a weak and selfish

mind; pathos, which is the whining of an unmanly spirit; and sublimity, which is the inflation of an empty head; when we consider that the great and permanent interests of human society become more and more the mainspring of intellectual pursuit; that, in proportion as they become so, the subordi- 5 nacy of the ornamental to the useful will be more and more seen and acknowledged, and that therefore the progress of useful art and science, and of moral and political knowledge, will continue more and more to withdraw attention from frivolous and unconducive to solid and conducive studies; that there- 10 fore the poetical audience will not only continually diminish in the proportion of its number to that of the rest of the reading public, but will also sink lower and lower in the comparison of intellectual acquirement; when we consider that the poet must still please his audience, and must therefore con- 15 tinue to sink to their level, while the rest of the community is rising above it; — we may easily conceive that the day is not distant when the degraded state of every species of poetry will be as generally recognized as that of dramatic poetry has long been; and this not from any decrease either of intel- 20 lectual power or intellectual acquisition, but because intellectual power and intellectual acquisition have turned themselves into other and better channels, and have abandoned the cultivation and the fate of poetry to the degenerate fry of modern rimesters, and their Olympic judges, the magazine 25 critics, who continue to debate and promulgate oracles about poetry as if it were still what it was in the Homeric age, the all-in-all of intellectual progression, and as if there were no such things in existence as mathematicians, astronomers, chemists, moralists, metaphysicians, historians, politicians, 30 and political economists, who have built into the upper air of intelligence a pyramid, from the summit of which they see the modern Parnassus far beneath them, and, knowing how small a place it occupies in the comprehensiveness of their prospect, smile at the little ambition and the circumscribed 35 perceptions with which the drivelers and mountebanks upon it are contending for the poetical palm and the critical chair.

NOTES.

1 1. After the title I have omitted the sub-title, "Part I." See notes on 45 6 and 45 21.

1 10. *The one is the τὸ ποιεῖν.* Cf. Sidney, *Defense* 6 30.

1 13. *The τὸ λογίζειν.* Shelley inadvertently substitutes an active for the proper deponent form.

1 24. *Shadow to the substance.* Cf. 24 14.

3 13-15. *The future . . . the seed.* Cf. 6 6-8 : " He beholds the future in the present, and his thoughts are the germs of the flower and fruit of latest time." And see 38 19-25.

4 28. *Unapprehended.* Cf. 11 21, 13 26, 46 25.

5 4-6. *The same footsteps,* etc. *De Augment. Scient.* cap. 1, lib. iii. (Shelley's note). Cf. *Adv. Learning* 2. 5. 3.

5 20-29. *But poets . . . religion.* Cf. Shelley, *Discourse on the Manners of the Ancients :* " For all the inventive arts maintain, as it were, a sympathetic connection between each other, being no more than various expressions of one internal power, modified by different circumstances, either of an individual or of society."

6 1. *Prophets.* Cf. Sidney, *Defense* 5 12-16.

6 14-15. *A poet participates in the eternal, the infinite, and the one.* Cf. the discussion in my edition of Sidney's *Defense of Poesy,* Introduction, p. xxix ff.

6 31-7 2. *But poetry,* etc. Cf. Plato, *Symposium* 205 (Shelley's trans.) : ". . . Poetry, which is a general name signifying every cause whereby anything proceeds from that which is not into that which is; so that the exercise of every inventive art is poetry, and all such artists poets. Yet they are not called poets, but distinguished by other names; and one portion or species of poetry, that which has relation to music and rhythm, is divided from all others, and known by the name belonging to all."

7 14. *Mirror.* Shelley is partial to this figure. Cf. 10 30-32, 18 16, 19 6 ff., 24 11, 46 26.

8 13-18. *Hence the language,* etc. Cf. Sidney, *Defense* 5 33-34, 11 25-31, 33 19-24.

8 19. *Hence the beauty of translation.* But cf. Goethe, *Dichtung und Wahrheit,* Th. 3, B. 11, quoted in Hayward, *Statesmen and Writers* 2. 307: "I honor both rhythm and rime, by which poetry first becomes poetry; but the properly deep and radically operative — the truly developing and quickening, is that which remains of the poet when he is translated into prose. The inward substance then remains in its purity and fulness; which, when it is absent, a dazzling exterior often deludes with the semblance of, and, when it is present, conceals."

8 30 ff. *Yet it is,* etc. Cf. Bagehot, *Literary Studies* 2. 351: "But the exact line which separates grave novels in verse, like *Aylmer's Field* or *Enoch Arden,* from grave novels not in verse, like *Silas Marner* or *Adam Bede,* we own we cannot draw with any confidence. Nor, perhaps, is it very important; whether a narrative is thrown into verse or not certainly depends in part on the taste of the age, and in part on its mechanical helps. Verse is the only mechanical help to the memory in rude times, and there is little writing till a cheap something is found to write upon, and a cheap something to write with. . . . We need only say here that poetry, because it has a more marked rhythm than prose, must be more intense in meaning and more concise in style than prose." And see also Hazlitt, *Lectures on the English Poets:* "I will mention three works which come as near to poetry as possible without absolutely being so; namely, the *Pilgrim's Progress, Robinson Crusoe,* and the *Tales of Boccaccio.* Chaucer and Dryden have translated some of the last into English rime, but the essence and the power of poetry was there before. That which lifts the spirit above the earth, which draws the soul out of itself with indescribable longings, is poetry in kind, and generally fit to become so in name, by being 'married to immortal verse.' If it is of the essence of poetry to strike and fix the imagination, whether we will or no, to make the eye of childhood glisten with the starting tear, to be never thought of afterwards with indifference, John Bunyan and Daniel Defoe may be permitted to pass for poets in their way." To these add Sidney, *Defense of Poesy* 11 18–22: "Which I speak to show that it is not riming and versing that maketh a poet — no more than a long gown maketh an advocate, who, though he pleaded in armor, should be an advocate and no soldier."

9 8–19. *Plato was essentially a poet,* etc. To the same effect in Shelley's Preface to his translation of Plato's *Symposium :* "Plato exhibits the rare union of close and subtle logic with the Pythian enthusiasm of poetry, melted by the splendor and harmony of his periods into one irresistible stream of musical impressions, which hurry the persuasions

onward as in a breathless career. His language is that of an immortal
spirit rather than a man. Lord Bacon is, perhaps, the only writer
who in these particulars can be compared with him; his imitator Cicero
sinks in the comparison into an ape mocking the gestures of a man."
Cf. also Sidney, *Defense* 3 27, note.

9 20. *Lord Bacon was a poet.* See the *Filum Labyrinthi,* and the
Essay on Death particularly (Shelley's note).

10 9 ff. *There is this difference,* etc. Cf. Aristotle, *Poetics* 9 1-3:
" The real distinction between the poet and the historian is not found
in the employment of verse by the former, and of prose by the latter,
for, if we suppose the history of Herodotus to be versified, it would be
nothing but history still, only now in a metrical form. The true ground
of difference is that the historian relates what has taken place, the poet
how certain things might have taken place. Hence poetry is of a more
philosophical and serious character than history; it is, we might say,
more universal and more ideal. Poetry deals with the general, history
with the particular. Now the general shows how certain typical characters will speak and act, according to the law of probability or of
necessity, as poetry indicates by bestowing certain names upon these
characters, but the particular merely relates what Alcibiades, a historic
individual, actually did or suffered." And see Sidney, *Defense* 18 25 ff.

10 27-29. *Hence epitomes,* etc. Cf. Bacon, *Adv. Learning* 2. 2. 4:
" As for the corruptions and moths of history, which are epitomes, the
use of them deserveth to be banished, as all men of sound judgment
have confessed, as those that have fretted and corroded the sound
bodies of many excellent histories, and wrought them into base and
unprofitable dregs."

11 4-5. *A single word even may be a spark of inextinguishable
thought.* Cf. 32 33-34 2: "Each is as a spark, a burning atom of
inextinguishable thought."

11 5-12. *And thus . . . images.* Cf. Sidney, *Defense* 4 5-15.

11 11. *Interstices.* Cf. 14 17, 39 28 ff.; also 41 13.

11 16-18. *Poetry is . . . with its delight.* Cf. Sidney, *Defense* 23 13-
25 2, 29 19-26.

12 3-7. *The poems of Homer,* etc. Cf. Sidney, *Defense* 2 27 ff.

12 7-8. *Homer embodied,* etc. Cf. Gladstone, *Gleanings* 2. 148:
" Lofty example in comprehensive form is, without doubt, one of the
great standing needs of our race. To this want it has been from the
first one main purpose of the highest poetry to answer. The quest of
Beauty leads all those who engage in it to the ideal or normal man, as
the summit of attainable excellence. . . . The concern of Poetry with

corporal beauty is, though important, yet secondary: this art uses form as an auxiliary, as a subordinate though proper part in the delineation of mind and character, of which it is appointed to be a visible organ. But with mind and character themselves lies the highest occupation of the Muse."

12 11. *Achilles, Hector, and Ulysses.* See Sidney, *Defense* 16 34–17 2: "See whether wisdom and temperance in Ulysses and Diomedes, valor in Achilles, friendship in Nisus and Euryalus, even to an ignorant man carry not an apparent shining."

13 13–14. *To temper*, etc. Cf. Sidney, *Defense* 58 3–5: "But if . . . you be born so near the dull-making cataract of Nilus, that you cannot hear the planet-like music of poetry."

13 23–24. *But poetry acts in another and diviner manner.* Cf. Jowett's words accompanying his translation of Plato, 2. 312–3 (2d edition): "In modern times we almost ridicule the idea of poetry admitting of a moral. The poet and the prophet, or preacher, in primitive antiquity are one and the same; but in later ages they seem to fall apart. The great art of novel writing, that peculiar creation of our own and the last century, which, together with the sister art of review writing, threatens to absorb all literature, has even less of seriousness in her composition. Do we not often hear the novel writer censured for attempting to convey a lesson to the minds of his readers?

"Yet the true office of a poet or writer of fiction is not merely to give amusement, or to be the expression of the feelings of mankind, good or bad, or even to increase our knowledge of human nature. There have been poets in modern times, such as Goethe or Wordsworth, who have not forgotten their high vocation of teachers; and the two greatest of the Greek dramatists owe their sublimity to their ethical character. The noblest truths, sung of in the purest and sweetest language, are still the proper material of poetry. The poet clothes them with beauty, and has a power of making them enter into the hearts and memories of men. He has not only to speak of themes above the level of ordinary life, but to speak of them in a deeper and tenderer way than they are ordinarily felt, so as to awaken the feeling of them in others. The old he makes young again; the familiar principle he invests with a new dignity; he finds a noble expression for the commonplaces of morality and politics. He uses the things of sense so as to indicate what is beyond; he raises us through earth to heaven. He expresses what the better part of us would fain say, and the half-conscious feeling is strengthened by the expression. He is his own critic, for the spirit of poetry and of criticism are not divided in him.

His mission is not to disguise men from themselves, but to reveal to them their own nature, and make them better acquainted with the world around them. True poetry is the remembrance of youth, of love, the embodiment in words of the happiest and holiest moments of life, of the noblest thoughts of man, of the greatest deeds of the past. The poet of the future may return to his greater calling of the prophet or teacher; indeed, we hardly know what may not be effected for the human race by a better use of the poetical and imaginative faculty. The reconciliation of poetry, as of religion, with truth, may still be possible. Neither is the element of pleasure to be excluded. For when we substitute a higher pleasure for a lower we raise men in the scale of existence. Might not the novelist, too, make an ideal, or rather many ideals of social life, better than a thousand sermons? Plato, like the Puritans, is too much afraid of poetic and artistic influences, though he is not without a true sense of the noble purposes to which art may be applied.

"Modern poetry is often a sort of plaything, or, in Plato's language, a flattery, a sophistry, or sham, in which, without any serious purpose, the poet lends wings to his fancy and exhibits his gifts of language and metre. Such an one seeks to gratify the taste of his readers; he has the '*savoir faire,*' or trick of writing, but he has not the higher spirit of poetry. He has no conception that true art should bring order out of disorder; that it should make provision for the soul's highest interest; that it should be pursued only with a view to 'the improvement of the citizens.' He ministers to the weaker side of human nature; he sings the strain of love in the latest fashion; instead of raising men above themselves he brings them back to the 'tyranny of the many masters,' from which all his life long a good man has been praying to be delivered. And often, forgetful of measure and order, he will express not that which is truest, but that which is strongest. Instead of a great and nobly-executed subject, perfect in every part, some fancy of a heated brain is worked out with the strangest incongruity. He is not the master of his words, but his words — perhaps borrowed from another — the faded reflection of some French or German or Italian writer, have the better of him. Though we are not going to banish the poets, how can we suppose that such utterances have any healing or life-giving influence on the minds of men?

"'Let us hear the conclusion of the whole matter': Art then must be true, and politics must be true, and the life of man must be true and not a seeming or sham. In all of them order has to be brought out of disorder, truth out of error and falsehood. This is what we mean by the greatest improvement of man. And so, having considered in what way ' we can best spend the appointed time, we leave the result with God.' "

13 27. *Poetry lifts the veil,* etc. The image of concealment and disclosure is a favorite with Shelley. Cf. 7 2, 9 29, 10 24, 12 13, 25–26, 29 ff., 18 17, 19 33, 20 16, 28 22, 30 5–6, 33 6–8, 41 14, 33, 42 1–2, 10–11, 16.

13 30. *And the impersonations,* etc. Cf. Sidney, *Defense* 30 20–25.

14 12–13. *Poetry enlarges,* etc. Cf. 9 22–24, 18 20–24; also 17 5. For the image cf. Bacon, *Adv. Learning* 1. 1. 3: "Nothing can fill, much less extend, the soul of man, but God and the contemplation of God."

14 21 ff. *A poet therefore would do ill,* etc. Cf. Forman, *Our Living Poets,* p. 50: "For a poem wherein the intimate tissues are thus qualified by an ante-natal religiousness, wherein the morality is not anatomical but cellular, there will always be (to follow up this analogy suggested by the high science of life) critical histologists to lay finger on this and that part, and announce to the untechnical the quality and meaning of the tissue; but such quality and meaning would often be knowledge as new to the poet's self as to the uninstructed audience — knowledge indeed as new as the chemistry of honey to the bee. . . . Doubtless the poet's mind would grasp and recognize the codification deduced from his work; but he would deny any intention that such codification should ever have been deduced — his proper role lying outside and around the considerations set forth by the critic."

15 20. *As.* This connective properly refers only to the former of the two preceding clauses.

16 7. *The drama had its birth.* For an excellent account of the Greek drama, see Moulton, *Ancient Classical Drama* (Macmillan, 1890).

16 16. *Idealisms.* Both Shelley and Peacock employ these abstracts in *-ism.* Cf. 17 28, 32 27, 53 37, 57 26, 58 21.

16 18. *Artists of the most consummate skill.* Cf. Shelley, *Discourse on the Manners of the Ancients:* " For it is worthy of observation that whatever the poets of that age produced is as harmonious and perfect as possible. If a drama, for instance, were the composition of a person of inferior talent, it was still homogeneous and free from inequalities; it was a whole, consistent with itself. The compositions of great minds bore throughout the sustained stamp of their greatness. In the poetry of succeeding ages the expectations are often exalted on Icarian wings, and fall, too much disappointed to give a memory and a name to the oblivious pool in which they fell."

17 6–7. *But the comedy should be as in King Lear, universal, ideal,*

and sublime. This is one of the profoundest sentences in the essay. Cf. the discussion in Sidney's *Defense of Poesy* 50 9, note.

17 20. *Calderon.* Cf. Shelley's letter to Peacock, Sept. 21, 1819 (Prose Works 4. 125; Peacock's Works 3. 436) : "I have read about twelve of his plays. Some of them certainly deserve to be ranked among the greatest and most perfect productions of the human mind. He excels all modern dramatists, with the exception of Shakespeare, whom he resembles, however, in the depth of thought and subtlety of imagination of his writings, and in the one rare power of interweaving delicate and powerful comic traits with the most tragic situations, without diminishing their interest. I rank him far above Beaumont and Fletcher." Again in a letter to Gisborne, Nov., 1820 (Prose Works 4. 193; Peacock's Works 3. 436) : "I am bathing myself in the light and odor of the flowery and starry *Autos.* I have read them all more than once."

17 25. *Observation.* 'Observance' is now appropriated to this special sense. Cf. S 26.

18 12–15. *The drama,* etc. Cf. Ruskin, *Crown of Wild Olive* (*War*) : "For it is an assured truth that, whenever the faculties of men are at their fulness, they *must* express themselves by art; and to say that a state is without such expression is to say that it is sunk from the proper level of manly nature."

18 28–29. *Even crime is disarmed of half its horror and all its contagion.* Cf. Burke, *Reflections on the Revolution in France* (Payne's ed. of Select Works 2: 89) : "Under which vice itself lost half its evil, by losing all its grossness."

19 1–2. *Self-knowledge and self-respect.* Cf. Tennyson, *Œnone :*

> Self-reverence, self-knowledge, self-control,
> These three alone lead life to sovereign power.

19 4. *The drama,* etc. This passage, like the well-known Shakespearean parallel (*Hamlet* 3. 2. 23–27), may be traced back to a saying attributed by Donatus to Cicero (Cicero, ed. Baiter-Kayser, 8. 228) : "Comœdiam esse imitationem vitæ, speculum consuetudinis, imaginem veritatis" [Comedy is the semblance of life, the mirror of custom, the image of truth].

20 2 ff. *Grossest degradation of the drama,* etc. Cf. Ward, *Hist. Eng. Dram. Lit.* 2. 613–4: "This absence of moral purpose is the true cause of the failure of our post-Restoration comic dramatists as a body to satisfy the demands which are to be made upon their art." Also 2. 620: "There are two forces which no dramatic literature can

neglect with impunity — the national genius and the laws of morality.
. . . Because, to suit the vicious license of their public, the contemporary comic dramatists bade defiance to the order which they well knew to be necessary for the moral government of human society, their productions have failed to hold an honorable place in our national literature."

20 10. *Comedy loses its ideal universality.* Cf. the anecdote related by Peacock (Memoirs of Shelley; Works 3. 411), which illustrates Shelley's sensitiveness to the exaggerations and perversions in which comedy sometimes abounds : " He had a prejudice against theatres, which I took some pains to overcome. I induced him one evening to accompany me to a representation of the *School for Scandal.* When, after the scene which exhibited Charles Surface in his jollity, the scene returned, in the fourth act, to Joseph's library, Shelley said to me : 'I see the purpose of this comedy. It is to associate virtue with bottles and glasses, and villany with books.' I had great difficulty to make him stay to the end. He often talked of the withering and perverting spirit of comedy. I do not think he ever went to another." Another illustration is furnished by Peacock (Works 3. 412): " When I came to the passage [Michael Perez's soliloquy in *Rule a Wife and Have a Wife*] . . . he said, ' There is comedy in its perfection. Society grinds down poor wretches into the dust of abject poverty, till they are scarcely recognizable as human beings; and then, instead of being treated as what they really are, subjects of the deepest pity, they are brought forward as grotesque monstrosities to be laughed at.' I said, ' You must admit the fineness of the expression.' ' It is true,' he answered, 'but the finer it is the worse it is, with such a perversion of sentiment.' "

21 13. *The bucolic writers.* Theocritus, Moschus, and Bion.

22 27. *Astræa.* Goddess of Justice. Cf. Ovid, *Metamorph.* 1. 150–1 : " Piety lies vanquished, and the virgin Astræa is the last of the heavenly deities to abandon the earth, now drenched in slaughter."

23 6. *Chain.* Cf. Plato, *Ion* 533, 536 (Shelley's trans.) : "It is a divine influence which moves you, like that which resides in the stone called magnet by Euripides, and Heraclea by the people. For not only does this stone itself possess the power of attracting iron rings, but it can communicate to them the power of attracting other rings; so that you may see sometimes a long chain of rings, and other iron substances, attached and suspended one to the other by this influence. And as the power of the stone circulates through all the links of this series, and attaches each to each, so the Muse, communicating through

those whom she has first inspired, to all others capable of sharing in the inspiration, the influence of that first enthusiasm, creates a chain and a succession. . . . Know then that the spectator represents the last of the rings which derive a mutual and successive power from the Heracleotic stone of which I spoke. You, the actor or rhapsodist, represent the intermediate one, and the poet that attached to the magnet itself. Through all these the God draws the souls of men according to his pleasure, having attached them to one another by the power transmitted from himself. And as from that stone, so a long chain of poets, theatrical performers and subordinate teachers and professors of the musical art, laterally connected with the main series, are suspended from the Muse itself, as from the origin of the influence. We call this inspiration, and our expression indeed comes near to the truth; for the person who is an agent in this universal and reciprocal attraction is indeed possessed, and some are attracted and suspended by one of the poets who are the first rings in this great chain, and some by another."

23 20. *Episodes.* Cf. 25 1.

25 1. *Quia carent vate sacro.* " Because they lack the bard divine." The reading of the original is: "Carent quia vate sacro " (Horace, *Od.* 4. 9. 28). Conington thus translates vv. 25–28:

> Before Atrides men were brave,
> But ah ! oblivion, dark and long,
> Has locked them in a tearless grave,
> For lack of consecrating song.

25 3–4. *Inspired rhapsodist.* Probably suggested by Plato's *Ion.* Ion himself, according to the dialogue, is such an inspired rhapsodist.

25 14. *Generals.* Shelley may still have been thinking of the *Ion.* Cf. *Ion* 540–1 (Shelley's trans.) :

Ion. I see no difference between a general and a rhapsodist.
Socrates. How! no difference ? Are not the arts of generalship and recitation two distinct things ?
Ion. No, they are the same.
Socrates. Must he who is a good rhapsodist be also necessarily a good general ?
Ion. Infallibly, O Socrates.

25 20–21. *The poetry of Moses, Job, David, Solomon, and Isaiah.* Cf. Sidney, *Defense* 9 19–24.

25 29. *Three forms.* Such a division is found in the Fourth Book of the *Republic.* Jowett (Plato 3. 57) says on this point: "The psy-

chology of Plato extends no further than the division of the soul into
the rational, irascible, and concupiscent elements, which, as far as we
know, was first made by him, and has been retained by Aristotle and
succeeding ethical writers. The chief difficulty in this early analysis
of the mind is to define exactly the place of the irascible faculty, which
may be variously described under the terms righteous indignation,
spirit, passion." This distribution of faculties is likewise observed in
the *Timæus;* cf. Jowett 3. 582: "The soul of man is divided by him
into three parts, answering roughly to the charioteer and steeds of the
Phædrus, and to the λόγος, θυμός, and ἐπιθυμία of the *Republic* and
Nicomachean Ethics. First, there is the immortal part which is seated
in the brain, and is alone divine, and akin to the soul of the universe.
This alone thinks and knows and is the ruler of the whole. Secondly,
there is the higher mortal soul which, though liable to perturbations of
her own, takes the side of reason against the lower appetites. The
seat of this is the heart, in which courage, anger, and all the nobler
affections are supposed to reside. . . . There is also a third or appe-
titive soul, which receives the commands of the immortal part, not
immediately but mediately, through the higher mortal nature." Another and fourfold division is found in the Sixth Book (*Rep.* 511;
Jowett 3. 399): "Let there be four faculties in the soul — reason
answering to the highest, understanding to the second, faith or persuasion to the third, and knowledge of shadows to the last." Else-
where (Plato 3. 77) Jowett translates the designation of the fourth
faculty as "the perception of likenesses."

26 1–3. *And the crow*, etc. Shakespeare, *Macb.* 3. 2. 51–3.

26 14 *Celtic.* Here, and wherever in the essay the word 'Celtic'
occurs, we should undoubtedly substitute 'Germanic.' Shelley's inad-
vertence is surprising.

27 9 ff. *The principle of equality*, etc. Cf. Plato, *Republic* 416–7
(Jowett's trans. 3. 294–5): "Then now let us consider what will be
their way of life, if they are to realize our idea of them. In the first
place, none of them should have any property beyond what is absolutely necessary; neither should they have a private house or treasury
closed against any one who has a mind to enter; their provisions
should be only such as are required by trained warriors, who are men
of temperance and courage; they should agree to receive from the
citizens a fixed rate of pay, enough to meet the expenses of the year
and no more, and they will go to mess and live together like soldiers
in a camp. Gold and silver we will tell them that they have from
God; the diviner metal is within them, and they have therefore no

need of the other earthly dross which passes under the name of gold, and ought not to pollute the divine by earthly admixture, for that commoner metal has been the source of many unholy deeds; but their own is undefiled. . . . And this will be their salvation, and the salvation of the State. But should they ever acquire homes or lands or moneys of their own, they will become housekeepers and husbandmen instead of guardians, enemies and tyrants instead of allies of the other citizens; hating and being hated, plotting and being plotted against, they will pass through life in much greater terror of internal than of external enemies, and the hour of ruin, both to themselves and to the rest of the State, will be at hand."

28 20–21. *Galeotto*, etc. " Galeotto was the book and he who wrote it." Dante, *Inf.* 5. 137.

28 22. *Petrarch*. Cf. Shelley's *Discourse on the Manners of the Ancients :* " Perhaps nothing has been discovered in the fragments of the Greek lyric poets equivalent to the sublime and chivalric sensibility of Petrarch."

28 33. *Vita Nuova*. Of this there are excellent translations by Rossetti, *Dante and his Circle*, and by Charles Eliot Norton.

29 7–8. *The most glorious imagination of modern poetry*. Cf. Shelley's *Discourse on the Manners of the Ancients :* " Perhaps Dante created imaginations of greater loveliness and energy than any that are to be found in the ancient literature of Greece."

29 18. *Dissonance of arms.* Cf. Longfellow, *The Arsenal at Springfield :*

> Peace ! and no longer from its brazen portals
> The blast of War's great organ shakes the skies !
> But beautiful as songs of the immortals,
> The holy melodies of love arise.

29 27–28. *The error which confounded diversity with inequality.* The truer doctrine has been expressed by Tennyson, *Princess* 7. 259–287 :

> For woman is not undevelopt man,
> But diverse ; could we make her as the man,
> Sweet love were slain ; his dearest bond is this,
> Not like to like, but like in difference.
> Yet in the long years liker must they grow ;
> The man be more of woman, she of man ;
> He gain in sweetness and in moral height,
> Nor lose the wrestling thews that throw the world ;
> She mental breadth, nor fail in childward care,
> Nor lose the childlike in the larger mind ;

> Till at the last she set herself to man,
> Like perfect music unto noble words;
> And so these twain, upon the skirts of Time,
> Sit side by side, full-summ'd in all their powers,
> Dispensing harvest, sowing the To-be,
> Self-reverent each and reverencing each,
> Distinct in individualities,
> But like each other ev'n as those who love.
>   . . . Seeing either sex alone
> Is half itself, and in true marriage lies
> Nor equal, nor unequal; each fulfils
> Defect in each, and always thought in thought,
> Purpose in purpose, will in will, they grow.

30 12. *Riphæus.* See Dante, *Paradiso* 20. 67–69, 118–124:

> Who would believe, down in the errant world,
> That e'er the Trojan Ripheus in this round
> Could be the fifth one of the holy lights?
> . . . Through grace, that from so deep
> A fountain wells that never hath the eye
> Of any creature reached its primal wave,
> Set all his love below on righteousness;
> Wherefore from grace to grace did God unclose
> His eye to our redemption yet to be,
> Whence he believed therein.

Cf. Plumptre's note on *Paradiso* 19. 70, in his translation of the *Divine Comedy:* " How can the justice of God be reconciled with the condemnation of the heathen who have sought righteousness, and yet have lived and died without baptism and in ignorance of the faith? Dante has no other solution than that of man's incapacity to measure the Divine justice. . . . It would be a miracle if Scripture presented no such problems. Man must believe that God is good and righteous in all his ways. If Dante does not go beyond this, we must remember that he at least placed the righteous heathen in a state in which there was only the pain of unsatisfied desire. . . . It is significant that his yearning after a wider hope grows stronger with his deepening faith towards the close of life."

Justissimus unus. *Æneid* 2. 426–7: " Rhipeus also falls, who was above all others the most just among the Trojans, and the strictest observer of right."

31 8–10. *And this bold neglect,* etc. Cf. 14 32–15 4.

31 14. *Laws of epic truth.* For these consult the *Poetics* of Aristotle.

32 1–2. *Limed the wings of his swift spirit.* See *Hamlet* 3. 3. 68–9:

> O limed soul, that, struggling to be free
> Art more engaged.

32 6. *Mock-birds.* Mocking birds.

32 7. *Apollonius Rhodius.* Flourished 250–300 B.C. He is best known by his *Argonautics*, a poem in four books (a translation in Bohn's Library). Cf. Mahaffy, *Hist. Grk. Lit.* I. 147–152, or his *Greek Life and Thought*, pp. 269–276.

32 8. *Quintus (Calaber) Smyrnæus.* Cf. Mahaffy, *Hist. Grk. Lit.* I. 153: " But we find no enduring result till the beginning of the fifth century, when an epic school was founded, principally in Upper Egypt, and of whom (*sic*) two representatives are well known — Nonnus and Musæus. There are several others mentioned in the fuller literature of the time. First, Quintus Smyrnæus (called *Calaber* from the finding there of the MS.), who wrote a continuation of Homer in fourteen books, thus taking up the work of the cyclic poets, who were probably lost before his time."

Nonnus. Mahaffy, *Hist. Grk. Lit.* I. 153: "Nonnus only, standing between the living and the dead, composing, on the one hand, his long epic on the adventures of Dionysus, and, on the other, his paraphrase of St. John's Gospel into Homeric hexameters, is a most interesting figure, though beyond the scope of the historian of Greek classical literature."

Lucan. Author of the *Pharsalia* (39–65 A.D.). See Cruttwell, *Hist. Rom. Lit.*, pp. 359–371.

Statius. Author of the *Thebaid*, and of an unfinished *Achilleid* (61–ca. 98 A.D.). Cruttwell, pp. 423–9.

32 9. *Claudian.* Close of fourth and beginning of fifth century A.D. Author of *Rape of Proserpine*, besides panegyrical and other poems.

33 16–21. *The age . . . invention.* Cf. Sidney, *Defense* 3 8–15.

34 27–30. *Let him spare to deface*, etc. Cf. Selkirk, *Ethics and Æsthetics of Modern Poetry*, pp. 205–6: "In the civilisation whose progress is thoroughly sound, the education of the head and of the heart should go abreast, and the assumed advancement in which poetry declines is more than likely to be the civilisation of an age that sacrifices its emotions to its reason. If this be true, we must be prepared to see a good many other things decline. First after poetry, perhaps religion, and after that the possibility of political cohesion. If we read history carefully enough, we shall find, in most cases, that this lopsided civilisation, under some very high-sounding aliases, ' Perfectibility of Human

Nature,' 'Age of Reason,' and so forth, has a trick of moving in a circle, and playing itself out. By-and-by the neglected half of human nature has its revenge. The fatal flaw in this emotionless culture is that it contains no sort of human amalgam strong enough to bind society together. The individual forces composing it are what Lord Palmerston would have called 'a fortuitous concourse of atoms,' and possess no element of political adherence. The forgotten thing that under the name of Emotion was allowed to fall asleep as quiet as a lamb — the busy worshippers of Reason taking no note of the fact — awakens one day with a changed name and a changed nature. It is now a lion. Spurned Emotion has grown to Rage, an easy transition. Renewed by his sleep, the lion rises up and scowls around him, rushes into society with his tail in the air, inaugurates a Reign of Terror, and reasserts the sovereignty of the brute. When the mad fit has gone, and the long arrears to the heart have been paid for in blood, cash down, society sits down again, clothed and in its right mind. The Sisyphus of civilisation finds himself again at the foot of the hill, glad to accept a philosophy that, if less high-sounding and pretentious, is at least a good deal more human."

35 2. *Exasperate.* In the etymological sense. Cf. *exasperation,* 37 28.

35 4–6. *To him that hath,* etc. An inexact quotation. See Mark 4. 25 : " For he that hath, to him shall be given; and he that hath not, from him shall be taken even that which he hath." Other forms, but none identical with Shelley's version, may be found in Matt. 13. 12 and 25. 29; Luke 8. 18 and 19. 26.

35 23–24. *The melancholy which is inseparable from the sweetest melody.* So in Shelley's *To a Skylark :*

> Our sincerest laughter
> With some pain is fraught;
> Our sweetest songs are those that tell of saddest thought.

And Shakespeare, *Merch. Ven.* 5. 1. 69 : " I am never merry when I hear sweet music."

35 27–28. *It is better to go,* etc. Another example of inexact quotation. See Eccl. 7. 2 : " It is better to go to the house of mourning, than to go to the house of feasting."

36 15. *The Inquisition in Spain.* Abolished in 1808, it was again revived by Ferdinand VII., and again suppressed in 1820, the year before Shelley wrote the *Defense.*

37 12–13. *I dare not,* etc. *Macbeth* 1. 7. 45.

38 2. *God and Mammon.* Matt. 6. 24: "Ye cannot serve God and mammon."

38 27–29. *As the odor,* etc. Cf. 8 19–21.

39 7. *A man cannot say,* "*I will compose poetry.*" Cf. Sidney, *Defense* 46 20–21: "A poet no industry can make, if his own genius be not carried into it."

39 25. *The toil and the delay,* etc. Such toil seems to be recommended by Dante; cf. his treatise *On the Vulgar Tongue,* Bk. 2, ch. 4 (Howell's trans.): "But these poets differ from the great poets — that is, the regular ones, — for these last have written poetry with stately language and regular art, whereas the others, as has been said, write by chance. It therefore happens that the nearer we approach to the great poets, the more correct is the poetry we write. . . . The proper result can never be attained without strenuous efforts of genius, constant practice in the art, and fully available knowledge. . . . And here let the folly of those stand confessed who, innocent of art and knowledge, and trusting to genius alone, rush forward to sing of the highest subjects in the highest style."

40 2. *Unpremeditated.* Milton (*P. L.* 9. 21–24) speaks of his "celestial Patroness,"

> Who deigns
> Her nightly visitation unimplored,
> And dictates to me slumbering, or inspires
> Easy my unpremeditated verse.

40 23–25. *It is as it were the interpretation of a diviner nature through our own.* Cf. Plato, *Ion* 533–4 (Shelley's trans.): "For the authors of those great poems which we admire do not attain to excellence through the rules of any art, but they utter their beautiful melodies of verse in a state of inspiration, and, as it were, *possessed* by a spirit not their own. Thus the composers of lyrical poetry create those admired songs of theirs in a state of divine insanity, like the Corybantes, who lose all control over their reason in the enthusiasm of the sacred dance, and during this supernatural possession are excited to the rhythm and harmony which they communicate to men. . . . For a poet is indeed a thing ethereally light, winged, and sacred, nor can he compose any thing worth calling poetry until he becomes inspired and as it were mad, or whilst any reason remains in him. For whilst a man retains any portion of the thing called reason, he is utterly incompetent to produce poetry, or to vaticinate. Thus those who declaim various and beautiful poetry upon any subject, as for instance upon Homer, are not enabled to do so by art or study; but every rhapsodist or poet, whether dithyrambic, encomiastic, choral, epic, or iambic, is excellent in proportion to the extent of his participation in the divine influence and the degree in which the Muse itself has descended on him. In other respects poets may be sufficiently ignorant and incapable. For they do not compose according to any art which they have acquired, but from the impulse of the divinity within them; for did they know any rules of criticism, according to which they could compose beautiful verses upon one subject, they would be able to exert the same faculty with respect to all or any other. The God seems purposely to have deprived all poets, prophets, and soothsayers of every particle of reason and understanding, the better to adapt them to their employment as his ministers and interpreters; and that we, their auditors, may acknowledge that those who write so beautifully are possessed, and address us inspired by the God. A presumption in favor of this opinion may be drawn from the circumstance of Tynnichus the Chalcidian having composed no other poem worth mentioning except the famous poem which is in every body's mouth, — perhaps the most beautiful of all lyrical compositions, and which he himself calls a gift of the Muses. I think you will agree with me that examples of this sort are exhibited by the God himself to prove that those beautiful poems are not human nor from man, but divine and from the Gods, and that poets are only the inspired interpreters of the Gods, each excellent in proportion to the degree of his inspiration. This example of the most beautiful of lyrics having been produced by a poet in other respects the worst seems to have been afforded as a divine evidence of the truth of this opinion."

41 5–8. *A word, a trait . . . will touch the enchanted chord.* Cf. Byron, *Childe Harold* Bk. 4, stanza 23:

> And slight withal may be the things that bring
> Back on the heart the weight which it would fling
> Aside for ever: it may be a sound —
> A tone of music — summer's eve — or spring —
> A flower — the wind — the ocean — which shall wound,
> Striking the electric chain wherewith we are darkly bound.

42 5–6. *The mind,* etc. *Paradise Lost* 1. 254–5.

42 19–20. *It creates anew the universe.* Cf. Sidney, *Defense of Poesy* 7 26–9 5.

42 23. *Words of Tasso.* Somewhat differently quoted in Shelley's letter to Peacock of 16th August, 1818, where it stands: *Non c'è in mondo chi merita nome di creatore, che Dio ed il Poeta.* In either

case the translation would be much the same: None merits the name of creator except God and the poet. Cf. Sidney, *Defense of Poesy* 8 27–30: "But rather give right honor to the Heavenly Maker of that maker, who, having made man to His own likeness, set him beyond and over all the works of that second nature."

43 7. *Confirm.* There is a variant reading, *confine.*

43 13. *" There sitting where we dare not soar."* Adapted from Milton, *P. L.* 4. 829:

> Ye knew me once no mate
> For you, there sitting where ye durst not soar.

43 21–31. This passage is framed out of Scriptural reminiscences. Some or all of the following sentences must have been present to Shelley's mind:

Dan. 5. 27. Thou art weighed in the balances, and art found wanting.

Isa. 40. 15. Behold the nations are as a drop of a bucket, and are counted as the small dust of the balance.

Isa. 1. 18. Though your sins be as scarlet, they shall be as white as snow.

Rev. 7. 14. Washed their robes, and made them white in the blood of the Lamb.

Heb. 9. 15. The mediator of the new testament, that by means of death, for the redemption of the transgressions that were under the first testament . . .

Heb. 12. 24. And to Jesus the mediator of the new covenant, and to the blood of sprinkling.

Matt. 7. 1. Judge not, that ye be not judged.

44 26. *The passions purely evil.* Shelley seems to have in mind some such classification of sins into lesser and greater as Dante adopts in the *Inferno.* The threefold division of Dante is into sins of I. Incontinence. II. Malice. III. Bestiality. Of these the former are regarded as the more venial, the latter as the more deadly. For the subdivisions, see Longfellow's Notes to the *Inferno*, the portion preceding the Commentary on Canto I., or Miss Rossetti's *Shadow of Dante*, ch. 5.

44 32. *A polemical reply.* To the essay of Peacock, for which see pp. 47–61.

45 6. *I, like them*, etc. This statement is illustrated by the following quotation from one of Shelley's letters to Peacock (Peacock's Works 3. 473; Shelley's Prose Works, Forman's edition, 4. 196–7):

"PISA, *March* 21, 1821.

"MY DEAR PEACOCK,—

"I dispatch by this post the first part of an essay intended to consist of three parts, which I design as an antidote to your 'Four Ages of Poetry.' You will see that I have taken a more general view of what is poetry than you have, and will perhaps agree with several of my positions, without considering your own touched. But read and judge; and do not let us imitate the great founders of the picturesque, Price and Payne Knight, who, like two ill-trained beagles, began snarling at each other when they could not catch the hare.

"I hear the welcome news of a box from England announced by the Gisbornes. How much new poetry does it contain? The Bavii and Mævii of the day are very fertile; and I wish those who honor me with boxes would read and inwardly digest your 'Four Ages of Poetry'; for I had much rather, for my own private reading, receive political, geological, and moral treatises than this stuff in *terza, ottava,* and *tremillesima rima,* whose earthly baseness has attracted the lightning of your undiscriminating censure upon the temple of immortal song. These verses enrage me far more than those of Codrus did Juvenal, and with better reason. Juvenal need not have been stunned unless he had liked it; but my boxes are packed with this trash, to the exclusion of better matter."

45 7. *Codri.* Codrus was perhaps a fictitious name. In any case a tragedy on the subject of Theseus is attributed to a certain Codrus, or, as some manuscripts read, Cordus, by Juvenal, who at the beginning of his First Satire speaks of the author and his production in terms of bitter railing (Juv. *Sat.* I. 1-2): "What! always a mere hearer? What, never to retort, bored as I am so often by the Theseid of Cordus hoarse with reciting?" See also the last note.

45 8. *Bavius and Mævius.* Associated together by Virgil, *Ecl.* 3. 90: "Let him that hates not Bavius, love your verses, Mævius." Mævius is likewise the object of Horace's detestation (Epode 10). In Smith's *Dict. of Greek and Roman Biography* it is said of them: "Bavius and Mævius, whose names have become a byword of scorn for all jealous and malevolent poetasters, owe their unenviable immortality to the enmity which they displayed toward the rising genius of the most distinguished of their contemporaries." See also note on 45 6.

45 21. *The second part.* This was never written.

45 31. *Low-thoughted.* An epithet borrowed from Milton, *Comus* 6: "low-thoughted care."

46 10 ff. *The persons,* etc. The thought seems to owe something to the arguments of Plato's *Ion.* See note on 40 23-25.

46 32. *Legislators.* Cf. 6 1-3.

INDEX OF PROPER NAMES.

ANALYSIS.

3. Creative poets and persuasive original philosophers practically identical, 9 33—10 7.

G. Superiority of poetry to history, 10 8—11 12.

     1. But the fragments of a history may be poetical, 10 33—11 12.

II. The Effects of Poetry, 11 13—33 26.

     A. Poetry gives delight, 11 16—12 7.

     B. Poetry is an instrument of moral improvement, 12 7—13 14.

         1. And this notwithstanding the moral conventionalities of his time and place, which the poet cannot help observing, 12 19—13 14.

     C. Poetry more efficacious for good than moral philosophy, 13 15—15 4.

         1. But poets must not moralize, in the restricted sense, 14 21—15 4.

     D. Historical review of European poetry, 15 5—33 26.

         1. Grecian poetry, 15 5—23 22.

             a. The perfection of the lyric and the drama at Athens will serve as the index of Athenian greatness in general, 15 5—21 8.

                 aa. The Athenian drama in the main superior to every other, 16 6—17 30.

                     a. Reservation in favor of tragicomedy; King Lear the most perfect specimen of dramatic art in the world, 17 2—30.

                 bb. The degeneracy of the drama always connected with the elimination of its poetry, 17 31—21 8.

                     a. The ennobling effects of the drama at its best estate, 18 12—19 12.

                     β. The decay of the drama accompanies the decay of social life; the Restoration plays are an example, 19 13—20 20.

                     γ. Necessity of regenerating the drama when it has been debased, 20 21—21 8.

             b. Inferiority of the Alexandrian writers, though creative imagination is not yet wholly extinct, 21 9—23 22.

         2. Roman poetry, 23 23—25 5.

             a. Poetry an exotic at Rome, 23 23—24 17.

             b. The Romans excelled rather in the poetry of action, 24 17—25 5.

D. The world could have dispensed with critics, reasoners, and political philosophers, but never with poets, 36 5–33.

E. At present, calculation has outrun conception, and deeds do not keep pace with knowledge, 37 1—38 2.

F. Poetry would give us an enlarged power over things, 38 3–15.

G. Poetry the centre, the life, the essence of all science, 38 16—39 5.

H. Poetry incapable of being produced at will, 39 5—40 13.

IV. The Diviner Sources and Effects of Poetry, 40 14—44 27.

A. Poets visited by transient inspirations, which, in recording, they transmute into immortal benefits to mankind, 40 14—41 21.

B. Poetry exorcises evil, enhances beauty, reconciles contradictions, banishes the commonplace, and creates the world anew, 41 22—42 24.

C. The poet, as poet, is the happiest, best, wisest, and most illustrious of men, 42 25—43 31.

　　1. But as man, being more susceptible to pain and pleasure, he is more sorely tempted than others, 43 32—44 23.

　　2. Still, the purely evil passions have little control over him, 44 24–27.

V. Concluding Observations, 44 28—46 32.

A. Digression concerning the particular occasion of the essay, 44 28—45 20.

B. Announcement of a second part, to be a defense of modern poetry in particular, 45 21–26.

C. This poetry likely to be the precursor of a new spiritual awakening to England, 45 26—46 3.

D. Poets the unconscious heralds of larger dispensations, 46 4–32.